JACINTHA

Also by Kathleen Winsor

FOREVER AMBER
STAR MONEY
AMERICA, WITH LOVE
WANDERERS EASTWARD,
WANDERERS WEST
CALAIS

KATHLEEN WINSOR
Jacintha

HARMONY BOOKS / NEW YORK

Published by Harmony Books, a division of Crown Publishers, Inc., One Park Avenue, New York, New York 10016 and simultaneously in Canada by General Publishing Company Limited.

HARMONY and colophon are trademarks of Crown Publishers, Inc.

Manufactured in the United States of America

This book has been previously published in different form as a novella entitled ON ROARING MOUNTAIN BY LEMONADE LAKE.

LIBRARY OF CONGRESS CATALOGING IN PUBLICATION DATA

Winsor, Kathleen.
Jacintha.

Rev. ed. of : On Roaring Mountain on Lemonade Lake.
I. Title.
PS3545.I7575J3   1984   813'.52   83-18583
ISBN: 0-517-55201-9 (pbk.)

Designed by Claudia Carlson
10 9 8 7 6 5 4 3 2 1
FIRST EDITION

To Roslyn Targ

JACINTHA

JACINTHA HAD CALLED OUT SEVERAL TIMES TO ASK THE driver to slow down, but apparently he did not hear, for they had dashed along recklessly ever since leaving the railroad station. She was not at all sure when that had been, but it seemed many hours ago.

Between bouncing up and down in the open-sided Concord coach, hanging onto its railing and clutching her hat, she had not had a chance to enjoy the country as she would have liked. They had been passing through the most magnificent, and astonishing, landscape she had ever seen.

For a time they had followed a broad, smooth-flowing river, meandering through yellow-green flowerless meadows set against pine-covered hills and, behind them, great rising mountains. They darted into a pine forest with a floor of tender green grass and purple-blue flowers, still and cool and murky, as if they had sunk far beneath the sea—then emerged suddenly upon a desolate area of gray white rocks, little yellow flowers, warped pine trees, and a vast terrace descending in broad steps over which poured steaming water, yellow and orange and rusty red. While she was still craning her neck, looking backward at that empty, cruel scene, she discovered that they were now hurtling through fields thick with sweet-smelling white and pink clover. Nearby was a steaming pool, subtly colored as an opal.

"Good heavens," murmured Jacintha, marveling. The coach bounded against a rock and her head struck the roof.

There were acres of white floating steam across great and small pools. They passed beneath a black bear in a tree, draped casually over flexed branches, and she gave a shriek of alarm as, leaning eagerly out, she looked directly up into his face and small, blinking eyes. Suddenly, a great gnarled, knotted cone of white crusty matter—like a sore on the earth, a wicked, painful boil of some kind— began to grumble and hiss, and water shot out of it thirty or more feet straight into the air. Jacintha turned to look back, hoping to see it happen again, but her driver was rushing furiously on. She had heard about these western coachmen and that it was all your life was worth to drive with one of them.

"I never should have come," she told herself for the tenth time. "God only knows how this will turn out."

The coach slowed down and came to a hard, jolting stop. Even that happened so suddenly that she was flung forward off the seat and had to grab the one in front to save herself from sprawling on the floor. She heard the driver's voice from outside where he sat on his perch above.

"You!" he bellowed. *"Out here!"*

Jacintha, adjusting the small bonnet set on top of her head, leaned forth and looked up at him, questioningly. "I'm not sure that I want to get out here," she said, after a moment. "Where are we?"

The driver jerked his head. "Roaring Mountain, by Lemonade Lake."

Jacintha moved to the other side of the coach and looked in the direction of his nod. Lemonade Lake, a small body of water to be called a lake, was directly before her. It was a strange yellowish green with many dead tree stumps sticking out of it at crazy angles, and its shore was bordered with stunted, unhealthy-looking pines.

Behind and beyond the lake was Roaring Mountain and, as Jacintha looked at it, her face sobered, losing its eagerly expectant look and turning serious, troubled, and reflective. There was nothing reassuring in the mountain's appearance; it was clearly an evil place of dire destiny and foreboding.

"I never should have come," she murmured again, her hand to her throat, then touching her lips with her fingers like a child to reassure herself.

The mountain was whitish, smoking and steaming everywhere, bare and rocky, with little wispy pines growing at random along the sides and top. Gnarled tree roots lay strewn about. It looked as if it had been ravaged by an enraged giant. After a moment Jacintha shook her head and settled back in the seat.

"Drive me somewhere else," she said.

"Get out!" shouted the driver. "You're expected!"

"I am?" she asked, tilting her head to one side. "How can that be? This is as much a surprise to me as anyone else. Well..." Apparently she must get out. She was not accustomed to being ordered about by anyone, much less a coachman, yet she knew that he would insist and that, eventually, she would be forced to obey. He did not offer to help, and she climbed down as gracefully as she could manage, with her long skirts and many petticoats. Then she stood beside the coach and unfurled her parasol. He was grinning at her, but his face was so ugly the grin seemed an unpleasant leer.

Jacintha bore the impertinence of his expression for a moment, wondering whatever had happened that she should find herself exposed to such insults. Then, haughtily, she raised her chin.

"I'm sorry I have nothing to give you," she said.

He was still grinning, and she would have liked to bash his head with the parasol. "Never mind," he retorted. "This is one of the few things in life you get free." Then he gave a roar of laughter.

Jacintha pretended to ignore him. "My baggage," she said. "You forgot it."

"It'll be along. Don't worry. In fact, you may as well stop worrying about everything." He swept down his whip with a flourish, the horses leaped forward, and the bright red coach with bright yellow wheels went flying away. Jacintha watched it disappear, which it did almost instantly, then turned once more to survey the mountain.

"Oh," she whispered finally, and chills crept over her, ending in a shudder. Sorrowfully she shook her head. "Ugly, ugly," she murmured.

Jacintha was herself extremely beautiful.

She was rather tall and her body was both slender and voluptuous. Her gown was new and very fashionable, though it had not been designed for traveling in this kind of country, an inconvenience resulting from the unexpected haste with which she had undertaken the journey. Bustles had lately gone out of style, and this dress was made in the new mode, fitting tightly over her breasts, waist, and hips, down to her thighs, with the skirt gathered up low in the back and garnished with ribbons and loops and fringe. It was made of stiff electric-blue taffeta with plum-colored ruffles around the skirt, plum-colored fringe, and much passementerie. There was a pleated flounce that kicked out flirtatiously above her pointed toes as she now moved slowly toward the mountain, still frowning.

Her bonnet had a small stuffed bluebird on it and was tied beneath her chin with a plum satin ribbon. She wore plum kid gloves and small diamond earrings.

Her face was patrician, smooth and white-skinned, with hair that was almost black and dressed in the new fashion—swept up off her neck, but for a few curling tendrils, with a mass of careless curls upon her forehead. Her eyes were large and dark brown, and their expression seemed both soft and brilliant; something in them implied that she simultaneously sought love and gave it, and because of this, men had adored her all her life. There was a delicate expectancy in her face, a hint of receptiveness. Every move or gesture was soft, fluid, gentle. She was a woman either gifted or practiced in the subtle art of pleasing and of evoking responsive, masculine admiration.

"How strange," she was saying softly, "that I should be in such a place as this at my time of life." Jacintha was twenty-five.

Still, here she was, and she had always been of a curious nature, eager as a child for investigation, retaining still the original capacity for honest wonder. She had always been ready for life and given it a warm welcome. She was not, and never had been, a coward, and that was probably the characteristic she most admired in herself.

Consequently, picking her way carefully over the uneven, squashy white earth, Jacintha walked around the edge of Lemonade Lake and took a few steps up the mountain. All day she had been noticing numbers of great, black, dismal-voiced birds that soared and flapped about and, when she asked the driver, had been told that they were ravens, common in these parts. She found to her surprise that it was difficult to breathe. The altitude here, he had said, was almost eight thousand feet, and she paused a moment to catch her breath. Depressed still by the morbid sight of Roaring Mountain, she turned her back on it and faced Lemonade Lake, across which, far beyond the meadow, stood a respectable pine-covered mountain.

Finally, when she could breathe easily again, she slowly turned around, lifting her skirts and glancing upward.

There stood a man, nearly naked, directly above her and not more than three feet away. She screamed and stumbled backward, almost toppling, then started down the mountainside as fast as she could go, her heart pounding, her high heels twisting in the rutted earth. She had taken only a few steps when she tripped and started to fall, her parasol flying out of her hands as she spread them frantically to catch herself.

At that instant he moved in front of her and she fell into his arms and against his chest where she remained for a second or two, afraid to look up. She had not actually seen him but gained only a horrified impression of a naked man, looming above her.

Now, all at once, she began a furious struggle to free herself. She had taken him to be an Indian in the brief glimpse she had of him and was sure that she was about to be scalped.

"Let me go!" she cried and, to her astonishment, he did so.

"Certainly," he said politely.

Amazed to hear him speak English, she stepped back and looked up at him. He was not an Indian, after all. At least, he was probably not an Indian, or perhaps only a half-breed. It was difficult to be sure since she had never seen an Indian. He was very tall, six feet three or four, and as he stood above her on the slope he seemed gigantic. His body—naked, for he wore only a loincloth—had the color and shine and apparent hardness of polished mahogany.

His chest was broad and imposing, swelling magnificently to his shoulders, narrowing sharply to his flat, muscled belly and symmetrical widespread legs. There was an awesome majesty about him as he stood, entirely unself-conscious, permitting her to look at him.

Jacintha was unaware that now she was gaping, astounded by this overpowering and gorgeous creature. Then, all at once, she realized that she had been staring and was horrified to imagine what he must think of her. She had never stared at a man like that in her life before. On the other hand, she had never seen one who looked as he did. That was no excuse, though. Her behavior had been shameful, and she could feel her face and throat burning with embarrassment.

"What a way for you to dress!" she chided.

At that, he threw back his head and burst into hearty laughter. Jacintha was hurt by the laugh, by her own feeling of having made herself ridiculous, the insults she had endured from the rude coachman, and her tiredness from the difficult trip. She would have found it restful to cry. And yet he was so entirely fascinating to her that even now, as he laughed, she watched him with her dark eyes wide and shining and intent, marveling.

For it was not merely the splendor of his body that astonished her; he was handsome in a manner so entirely reckless and virile that he created the instant impression of being resistless, incontestable. His eyes were black, his hair black, his teeth straight and startlingly white. He wore an Indian headdress of white and red feathers, spreading enormously, falling down his back to the ground. The impression he created was of great extravagance. He was so much of everything—strength, power, arrogance—that he seemed the essence of the very concept of masculinity.

He is *beautiful,* she thought. My God, but he's beautiful. Where did he come from and what's he doing here? What, as far as that goes, am *I* doing here?

"Did you come by way of Wraith Falls?" he inquired now, a challenging smile on his face.

"I don't know. Some repulsive creature in a Concord coach drove me. I expected to have my neck broken."

He laughed again. "That must have been Grant. He always drives like a demon." He shrugged. "After all, why shouldn't he?" Now he was smiling at her and Jacintha smiled back, though she had no idea what was supposed to be amusing. She smiled to please him, in response to him.

To her surprise she found that she was no longer frightened, not even tired, but was enjoying herself. This was certainly as exciting an adventure as any she had ever had, and this nearly naked man, whoever he was, stimulated her interest and admiration as no other man had ever done: there was both danger and fascination in him. She felt, as she stood and looked up at him, as though her nerves had been strung taut and set gently vibrating. She was tremendously exhilarated—yet there must be something sinister about him to have elicited such a response less than two minutes after she had first seen him.

All about and above them the whispering steam drifted and swirled. There was a strong, unpleasant sulfurous odor in the air, which now and then blew across her face and caused her nostrils to flare with delicate resentment. The sky was unnaturally blue and full of thick white clouds.

"It's strange," she said, when they had stood looking at each other for several moments and she had begun to feel dizzy. "I know we've never met before—yet you look familiar to me."

"Of course," he said, matter-of-factly. "You've known me all your life."

"I have?"

"Certainly. Each one draws a personal, private picture of the Devil."

"Oh."

The dizziness turned to a sick sinking in her stomach. She had known where she was ever since she got off the train this morning and that nasty, grinning man approached and offered to drive her in the coach. But she had continued to hope that she was having a nightmare and would presently awaken in her own bed at home.

I'm dead, then. My life is over. I shall never— She gave a sudden horrified gasp. *I will never see my children again!* She had two children, a boy and a girl, the boy four years old and the girl two. They were the prettiest, sweetest children imaginable. She had cherished and adored them more than anything in the world—except, perhaps, Brian.

And I will never see Brian again, either.

Her gloved hand was against her mouth, her eyes staring. She did not see him now—or even remember that he still stood there, watching her. She closed her eyes and shook her head and a slow, heavy despair seemed to plunge through her body, emptying it of hope, leaving only a desperate despondency that rose swiftly, flooding her entire being and sweeping her away helplessly into a bitter sea of grief and nostalgia.

For those things to be over—those parts of my life that I took so entirely for granted, as it seems now—

Her eyes still closed, she looked inward, and back. She discovered herself, with the two children, in their nursery at night. She spent a good deal of time with them, more than most women of her position did, and the happiest hour of the day came just before they went to bed. It was more precious to her than all others, she sometimes thought, because it must last her until they woke in the morning. Her husband would usually join them for a few minutes, but he was not disposed to be present for very long at a time. Jacintha did not mind this, understanding that men were likely to be more interested in the fact of a child's existence than in prolonged association with it. In fact, she was pleased that his interest in them was so entirely perfunctory. Had it been otherwise, she might have resented an encroachment upon her exclusive possession of their babyhood. It was her joy and privilege to have them press against her, to kiss and fondle them, to watch them at play and enter their games with them. *Flesh of my flesh*—she understood that with passionate, grateful intensity.

And yet, sometimes, sitting on the floor in her

dressing gown, while she read or told them a story, a strange premonition would arise, as if a silent figure had entered the room and beckoned her: *This will end.* She would draw them closer, telling herself that she must not be foolish and superstitious, that the premonition was nothing but her own reluctance to accept that they must someday grow up and leave her.

There, with her children, she was one woman.

With Brian, she seemed quite another. The tenderness and devotion carried across to her feeling for him, but it seemed of a different nature, entirely.

Jacintha had been surprised at the discovery of an eager sensual appetite within herself. It had been in hiding, apparently, for most of her life—through the conception and birth of her two children—and then one day it had simply appeared and altered her life completely, as if, after years of observing her surroundings through a blur, she had suddenly been given a new vision that changed the shapes and colors of her entire environment.

"You'll never know," she had told him, the first time it happened, "what it is you have done for me."

She lived for the moments of their privacy, recalling them, evoking them; her memories were extraordinarily vivid. There seemed no possible satiation, and she was always reluctant to leave him and go about her ordinary life. He engrossed her so completely that she had no moment of absolute freedom from him, nor did she want it. She clung to his image with a kind of desperation, as if she were not even yet entirely convinced of her good fortune. If their eyes met across a drawing room filled with polite people, Jacintha sensed an imminent collapse of the world, so powerful and vast did their infatuation seem.

Now—these things were gone.

She did not cry as she stood there on Roaring Mountain, her head bowed, her eyes closed. No tears, apparently, were made available for one's own death. Tears were joined to hope; they could fall at pain or disappointment, releasing tensions and thereby altering the gravity of one's emotions. But nothing like that was possible now.

He had stood watching her silently. As she raised her head and looked at him once more, he regarded her soberly, almost sympathetically.

"All newcomers feel as you do," he told her quietly. "There is a terrible torment when they realize that life is over. Whatever was sweet becomes sweeter, of course."

Jacintha slowly shook her head. "I'll miss my children most of all."

"Perhaps I can console you a little. There's a saying you may have heard that there can't be any Hell because in two weeks everyone would get used to it. Well, in a couple of weeks, or less, you'll be so taken up with what's going on here that you will scarcely remember your former life. All the people you knew then will seem vague and unreal, as if you had only imagined them."

Jacintha listened, but her expression was dubious. "Really?"

He smiled. "Really."

She looked around. All about them the glaring white

mountains steamed and whispered. Here and there were smears of bright yellow sulfur. Shallow lukewarm streams trickled over white and greenish beds. Farther up the mountainside were many knoblike terraces, one above another, with reddish-brown rocks covering each knob; dead trees stuck up amid the red-brown ruin.

"I can't imagine anything at all going on here," she said dismally. "It's much too dreary and there isn't another soul in sight."

"This is only part of it, after all. You've come to a place which is infinite. In spite of the size, people will turn up, I assure you. Coincidence is the law—even here."

Jacintha was peculiarly aware that what he had predicted was, in a sense, beginning to happen already. The terrible despondence had begun to lessen and she was actually taking an almost lively interest in her surroundings—and in this splendid, indomitable man who confronted her.

Her interest in him was sufficiently acute that she found herself growing angry with him for standing there naked and beautiful, so constant a temptation that she longed to cover her eyes with her hands and demand that he put on something decent before she would trust herself to look at him again.

"Whatever makes you go around like that?" she demanded suddenly, her voice irritable and anxious.

He smiled, understanding, apparently, why she asked. "It's the only sensible getup for this part of the country. After all, should I wear horns and a tail and cloven hooves just because some nervous old maid thought that would do me for a costume?''

Jacintha burst into a sudden shocked little laugh, since that was a new slant on the subject for her.

"Why!" she cried. "You have a sense of humor!"

"That's one of my vices." He sat down then, spreading his legs wide apart and resting his elbows on his knees. He gestured for her to sit beside him, but Jacintha declined.

"No, thanks. I'm afraid I'd soil my gown."

He shrugged. "I've never yet seen a tourist who was suitably dressed. You all wear the goddamnedest rigs." His eyes were appraising her slowly, amused, it seemed, by her beautiful and fashionable gown.

"How can we be suitably dressed when we come here at such short notice—and have no idea what we'll find when we arrive?" She was glancing around once more. "In fact, this looks like a caricature of what I expected Hell to be. This mountain does have a malevolent look to it, and certainly Lemonade Lake could be a pool of poison—but all around is the most innocent and delightful mountain scenery. It really isn't so very terrible, you know," she added, turning back once more as if to inform him of something he might not have realized.

He was still watching her, his face speculative, his eyes continuing to rove over her body, so that she wondered if it was one of his attributes to be able to see through a woman's clothing. Very likely it was. A proper Devil should be equipped with all the traits a man would like to have.

"No," he agreed after a moment. "But were you damned for anything very terrible?"

Jacintha opened her eyes wide. "Don't *you* know why I'm here? Aren't you the one who decides which of us is damned and which is saved?"

He laughed. "Of course not. It is your contemporaries who determine your fate. And, may I add, they keep me well supplied with companions of all kinds—some of them much too dull and respectable for my tastes, but apparently guilty in the eyes of their friends."

"Oh," murmured Jacintha, "I don't like this. I'd rather—"

"You'd rather I were the culprit?"

"Yes. Yes, I think I would. That's what I was always taught, at least."

"You will find, my dear young lady, that you were taught a great deal of rubbish. What is your name, by the way?"

"Jacintha. Jacintha Frost."

"Pretty—and rather odd, too, isn't it? All you Victorians have exotic names."

"I have always liked it," said Jacintha proudly.

"I'm sure you do. Tell me how you happen to be here. I'm curious about you: you don't look a sinner to me."

"I am, though. I sinned grievously." She heard her voice take on a solemn, churchgoing tone. Then, with conscious effort, she reverted to her natural sound, soft and light and caressive, one of her greatest charms and a quality Brian had never ceased praising. She drew a deep breath. "I am here because of a crime of passion—two, in fact: my passion for another man, and my husband's when he discovered me."

"Caught you in flagrante?" At that he smiled maliciously, and Jacintha was sure that he had a very clear picture in mind.

"Of course not!" she said sharply, rebuking him. "He found a letter Brian had written me. I was a fool to have kept it, yet I thought my husband was an honorable man. I had no idea he would sneak through my possessions."

He laughed again. "And what happened then?"

"He shot me." Suddenly she stopped, frowning a little, with puzzlement rather than anger. She looked at him. "Did you hear what I said just then?"

He lifted his head, squinting against the sun, smiling. "Yes, I heard you. You said that he shot you." From somewhere or other he had taken a small pocketknife and now, picking up a piece of wood, he began to whittle at it, rapidly peeling and shaping it, turning it this way and that to study his handiwork and, with his leftover attention, glancing now and then at Jacintha. "Isn't that what you said?"

"Yes," she replied softly. "I did. But how is it possible?"

"He must have done *something* drastic—since here you are."

Jacintha looked at what he was whittling and was

alarmed to see a cross, to which he was now adding a figure. He worked with such precision that it was clear he was a practiced and talented craftsman. She wanted to tell him to stop, that he was being blasphemous, but did not dare. Instead, she looked down to where her fingers twisted the silk cords on her handbag.

"But the way I said it—so casually—as if it were nothing at all. As if I had forgotten already what it was like to have him come into the room and stand there staring at me without a word until my flesh began to crawl and I knew he had somehow found out— And then—!" She stopped, gave a low moan, and covered her face with her hands. She stood shivering, overcome with reminiscent terror as slowly, once more, she turned and saw the look on her husband's face.

She had felt as if she were in the midst of a nightmare, where every effort to save herself, to scream or run or force herself to waken had proven impossible. She was weighted by her guilt, knowing that her expression betrayed her and that she would, if he desired, betray herself even further. An inexorable force rushed her toward disaster.

"Good evening," he said.

Jacintha tried to answer but found her lips paralyzed. She nodded, though even that required tremendous effort and was scarcely perceptible.

He was across the room from her. Between them lay the rich and elegant bedchamber, furnished in the fashionable Louis Quatorze style, with carved and gilded ceiling, walls of tufted red brocade, handsome sweeping velvet draperies, flowers and books and crystal lamps.

He did not come any nearer but continued to stare at her.

Jacintha stared back, scarcely able to see him, for her terror was so great that her vision had blurred, as though she stood in deep water. *He's going to kill me. I will never see Brian or the children again. Nothing I can do will stop him. He is bent on murder.* She had a swift vision of her two children in their charming Kate Greenaway clothes, running to greet her.

They continued facing each other, motionless, silent.

At last, he slowly lifted his hand and she watched while it moved toward the inner breast pocket of his coat. Jacintha gasped and, the next moment, heard herself scream. He drew forth an envelope, and now he was smiling. The smile had been more horrifying than the knowledge that he was about to kill her. How could she have imagined that this man—with whom she had lived for five years and who had been, at least, a devoted, if not a tender husband, to whom she had borne two children— how could this man be capable of such evil?

In another moment she realized that this smile had always been his potentiality, that, in a sense, he had been smiling at her in this way during all the years of their marriage and that she had hated him all along for knowing him capable of such cruelty. She also understood that she had fallen in love with Brian in part, at least, because she despised her husband.

"Why did you scream?" he asked her, as he continued to smile. He was enjoying this moment, her terror and guilt, his power, far more than he had ever enjoyed an affectionate moment between them. "You thought, perhaps, that I was reaching for a gun and that I would shoot you. No—not just now, at least. This, I believe, is an envelope you will recognize."

She felt an uncanny terror, produced not by his revelation of the letter, but by her own perception that it was his intention to torment her—to let her beg and plead for her life, while he rejoiced in her degradation. Then, once she began to believe that he might let her live, he would kill her.

"I know you too well, Martin," she said slowly, "not to discern exactly what thoughts and intentions your face is reflecting." Her chin was up now and she was panting, but with excitement and pride, not fear or remorse. She faced him squarely, her breasts raised high, her arms falling to her sides; and her voice rang out in a strong, clear tone: "Of course I recognize the envelope! There were many others—I kept only that one, because I thought it the most beautiful!"

The effect was instantaneous. His sense of power crumpled, and he stood staring back at her with the sickly look of a caught criminal.

"I do love Brian—and I do not love you. If you don't kill me, I shall continue to see him, and nothing you can do will stop me. I knew a moment ago when I saw that twisted smile that I never really loved you at all—"

She had an exultant moment of triumph, a conviction

that she had torn all power from him and forced him to act without any of the cruel pleasures he had expected to derive from her murder. She continued to face him proudly, as his hand reached once more to his breast pocket, brought forth the pistol, and leveled it at her. . . .

"And now I am here," she concluded, telling her story's ending to the Devil.

He gave a sigh, though she could not tell if it came from boredom or sympathy. Then he flipped the whittled cross aside and stood up. Shutting one eye, he took aim with his knife and shot it into a tree trunk several yards distant, where it stuck and quivered.

"It's a common enough story," he said. "You'd be surprised how many adulteresses turn up here." He smiled at her. "I like that word: adulteress. Amusing, isn't it?"

Jacintha haughtily raised her chin. "You may call it amusing. It cost *me* my life."

"Yet you must have known it would. After all, there are few things more aggravating to a husband than to have his wife in love with another man. And you did keep the letter. You've just told me how well you knew him, how you could read his thoughts from his expressions. If you knew him that well, then you knew that he would find it someday and, when he did, would kill you. I think you wanted to die."

"*What?*" Jacintha took a step or two backward and stared at him with an expression of outraged horror. "How dare you say such a thing!"

"Now, now," he said softly. "It was not an accusation. Not unless you think so. Anyway, there's very little difference between being dead because you wished to be and dying because you could not help yourself. And, of course, I played my own part in your untimely demise, as you earthlings call it.''

"You played a part? What part could you possibly have played?''

"Don't you know that when a woman commits adultery, it is the Devil who puts his penis into her—and that it emerges from her husband's head as two horns? Or has that superstition ended?''

Jacintha felt her face turn hot. She opened her fan and began to flutter it nervously. She had never heard such talk; it was disgraceful. She did not know what to do, where to look, what to reply. She should have pretended that she did not even know what he meant, but it was too late for that now.

He watched her a moment. Then he threw back his head and roared with laughter. "Oh!'' he groaned. "Oh, my God!''

Jacintha glared, as if she could make him ashamed of himself, but when he ignored her and only continued his ribald guffaws, she turned and began carefully making her way back down the slope of Roaring Mountain. She returned to the edge of Lemonade Lake and, her folded fan pressed thoughtfully against her chin, stood gazing into the lake's opaque surface, trying to regain her composure.

Too much had happened during the past few hours. She felt dizzy and bewildered, unsure of herself.

But worst of all was this...Devil—for she found it almost impossible to think of him as what he was, and that, she knew, must be the result of some fatal trick he had. She must guard against him, as she had always been warned to do. She must not permit him to gain a victory over her. She must be more alert than ever, for he undoubtedly had formidable and mysterious magic at his command.

Even now, she could feel it working.

At this very moment, she longed to turn and look at him. Had she merely wished to glance, to see where he was or what he was doing, she would have followed her inclination. But this feeling was not so simple. In a matter of seconds it had grown persistent, tormenting and tantalizing her, until she had a sudden horrified glimpse into the sensation of gluttony. She felt overwhelmed by some merciless hypnotic spell.

Jacintha was terrified, and violently excited.

She whirled suddenly and confronted him, only a few feet away, then timidly smiled.

To her dismay, she found the sight of him reassuring, quelling her anxiety. It was as if she had become dependent on him, convinced that he had deserted her and would not be there when she turned around.

The rhythm of his body, walking slowly toward her, created the weird sensation of her veins being filled with quicksilver.

He was elemental and spectacular beyond any dream she had ever had. She gazed at him now with the candid, unashamed awe of a child. But only for a moment. Then she was embarrassed, because of both his nakedness and her own avid pleasure in his beauty. She began to tap the pointed toe of her right shoe at a furious rate.

He was standing beside her again.

She waited, breathing faster, feeling both foolish and helpless, trying to think of something to say. She knew that he was teasing her, but found herself at a loss as to how she should behave with him.

Then, with sudden recklessness, she threw back her head and looked up into his face, allowing him the full vision of her beauty. Her pink, soft mouth was slightly open, so that the even edges of her teeth showed. Her head tilted so far back that her eyes were partly closed. Her skin, in the strong sunlight, was almost luminous. There was a lyric, warm, opulent quality to her face and manner that had been greatly disturbing to every man she had known. Now, still gazing up at him from beneath her black lashes, she let her nostrils flare slightly.

Jacintha intended, as she turned her face upward, for him to concentrate on her beauty and thereby lose himself. Instead, she found that her own energy and interest drew slowly into focus and centered on his mouth, which was full and sensual, yet sensitive as the work of a fine artist. She began to wonder how his mouth would feel upon her own and whether he would be as violent in love as his vibrancy seemed to promise.

Moments passed. Gradually, his face blurred until she could see nothing but his mouth, lips slightly parted, slightly smiling. Her eyes felt heavy and weighted and her lids began to fall and, though she seemed to struggle for a long while to keep them open, at last she gave up and they closed.

Very, very slowly, as if she moved in a dream or underwater, she felt herself begin to sway forward. There seemed some compelling force at work, subjecting her to a massive and alien will. Though he stood, in reality, only a few inches from her, she sensed herself moving endlessly through space and then, after a long while, her body touched his. She felt one arm go about her waist to hold her steady, and she waited for whatever was going to happen—relieved of all personal responsibility, since his power was incontestable. Passively, as though she drifted on a vast surface of water, she waited.

Then, in an instant, she realized what had happened.

She had been tempted.

She jabbed him roughly, and he let her go. He was smiling again.

"For a moment I felt faint; I don't know what happened." She stared at him challengingly.

He nodded, still watching her with a look of amusement. Several moments passed in silence, before he said:

"You've been looking at me for some time."

"Yes," she admitted calmly. "I suppose I have. You're the most beautiful man I've ever seen." She paused, listening it seemed, to some other Jacintha, known to her long ago, who had been speaking those same words, but . . . to another man.

Brian?

All at once she reached out with one hand, fingers

spread, and touched his chest, with its light covering of black curls. The touch was brief, little more than a gesture.

"Why, you're warm. And you are beautiful. I was told the Devil was ugly. Are you sure you're not an impostor?"

"I'm sure."

She grew more thoughtful, observing him with earnest attention, even a kind of wistfulness. "You won't make me fall in love with you?"

"I won't try to."

"I was warned long ago to beware of love."

He was smiling, gently teasing. It seemed he knew what she was going to say before she did.

Still, she continued. "My mother consulted a gypsy, I've been told, when I was four months old. She looked at me carefully, examined my fingers and toes, and pronounced to my mother: 'Let her beware of love.' "

"She was right. You should have remembered it. But you fell in love with Brian. Why?"

"At first, it was the way he looked. And later, it was because he gave me pleasure—great pleasure—"

He laughed softly, as if at a bitter joke. "Pleasure is the easiest thing to come by in your world. Far easier than a good dinner."

"Perhaps," she reminded him loftily, "but you are in no position to form an opinion on that subject."

"Am I not? That is, perhaps, the one subject on which I *am* best qualified to speak."

"Pleasure is a mortal sin. You are immortal." She

glanced at him doubtfully. "Aren't you?"

"I am. Unluckily."

"I've sometimes wondered, what do the immortal gods find in mortal women?"

There was another long silence. "Mortality."

Jacintha turned quickly away. After a moment, she glanced around at him, over her shoulder, from the corners of her dark eyes. "Mortal women tempt you. But you do not fall in love with them? Ever?"

"I hope you're willing to permit me a few advantages in my dubious predicament."

"But suppose something happened?"

"Do you mean, suppose a woman became of great importance to me?"

"Yes," Jacintha said earnestly. "A woman became of the greatest importance. What then? Suppose you got trapped among us—became, in a sense, one of us?"

"There is no such chance. That is my burden for however long time may last. However, I would willingly give up immortality for those few hours of sensuality."

"How strange. Why do you do it?"

He was smiling reminiscently, almost tenderly. "Because," he told her softly, "it is glorious."

"For you, too?" Jacintha asked wonderingly.

He laughed. "Did you mistake me for a philanthropist?"

"And still you never fall in love," she repeated regretfully. This seemed a bitter piece of news.

"The fact is—I cannot."

Jacintha sighed. *Oh, dear, whatever has become of me? I am a sinner; I've come to the right place.*

Guiltily she pictured Brian, at this very moment, grieving and heartbroken. She hung her head slightly, as if bowing beneath self-castigation, then, as she shook her head from side to side, her eyes shifted unexpectedly and she glanced down at the loincloth that barely covered him.

"You weren't sure I had one?"

Her glance had been so swift, so covert—how had he seen it? Angrily she looked up at him. "I don't know what you're talking about! I haven't been dead twenty-four hours and you're making fun of me!"

As she talked, her eyes flashing and her face lively and intense, he watched her, still smiling. He made her feel as though she were an amusing, inconsequential child. How strange and wicked it was for a man to lack respect for women.

"You Victorians," he said, shaking his head. "I think I'll be glad when there's a new age and a different kind of woman begins to show up around here. Of course," he added, "you are womanly women—totally without logic."

"How dare you!" Before she realized what she was doing, she raised one fist and began pounding at his chest. "I won't permit you to talk to me like that!"

He caught hold of her wrist and lightly twisted her arm to one side, then turned, flattened his lips against his teeth, and gave a shrill, piercing whistle.

Jacintha was crying softly, a mournful little sound.

"Keep quiet!" he spoke sharply. "Did you expect I would turn out to be like all the men you've known—considerate and tolerant of the whimsies of a creature clever enough to have herself treated like a goddess? You can consider that part of your life over, along with the rest of it. Things go the way I like them here—I consider no one's wishes or preferences but my own."

"Well!"

At that moment Jacintha heard a sound like thunder and, while she stood listening, a great, shining black horse came galloping toward them. He was not saddled, but only bridled. He came at a furious rate, and Jacintha watched him with wonder and awe, for she had never seen so superb an animal. He slowed his pace abruptly as he approached and stopped beside them, his gleaming black sides heaving and quivering.

The Devil jerked his head. "Climb on."

"I will not!" She gave him a look of alarm. What kind of place would he take her to? She was afraid of him now.

Almost before she knew what was happening he had placed his square-fingered hands about her narrow waist and hoisted her sideways onto the stallion's back. With a swift leap he was behind her, his arm passed about her body, drawing her against him, and the horse was off at a gallop.

Jacintha hung onto her hat with one hand and her beaded bag and fan with the other. The horse went rushing along, moving with a swift tread that was strangely light for so great an animal. Jacintha, during the first few moments, was wholly occupied with this new sensation of height and bewildering speed, as though she had been lifted off the earth by some unseen force and was now being blown through space against her will. Suddenly she felt her hat snatched from under her clutching hand and looked frantically around to see it go sailing away. She gave a cry of protest as her bag and fan were wrenched from her other hand and flung into the distance.

"Stop!" she cried. "My hat! My—"

"Stop worrying about your damned trinkets and enjoy the ride. Look around you. This is magnificent country. I designed it myself." He smiled. "Stop staring at me—and look at it."

Jacintha obeyed. He was the first man she had known who undoubtedly meant what he said.

The ride was exhilarating, with the movement of the fleet, swift, flowing animal beneath them, and the feeling of his body against her back, holding her against him, his spread hand upon her belly, warming and vitalizing.

Now that she knew this was his handiwork, she looked about her with even greater interest than on the ride from the railroad station. He pointed out a distant herd of grazing buffalo and two or three elk feeding chest-deep in succulent grass. They sped through fields of pink and purple and blue flowers, passing numerous showy magpies, whose feathers appeared to be comically loose and floppy.

But amid all this natural, innocent beauty rose weird

and awful sights. Whichever way she looked, nature seemed out of kilter. That was his idea, no doubt, of a joke. They passed steaming waterfalls, pouring over orange rock. The stallion plunged into a meadow, and they found themselves splashing and floundering through boiling, shallow streams rushing by in all directions, enveloping them in sulfur-laden clouds. There were bubbling, brilliant blue pools, surrounded by halos of blue steam; and dead trees, black at the top, white at the bottom, that looked like the petrified legs of giant horses from which the bodies had decayed and fallen away. There was a yellow terrace overrun with hot, hissing water.

All at once, feeling suddenly gay and reckless, Jacintha turned her head and looked up at him. "It does look like Hell!" she cried joyously, and they both burst into laughter. She started to turn back again but found herself caught, gazing at his mouth once more, her senses swirling and bemused by the feeling of his body, the pressure of his hand, the glittering light of his black eyes.

"Wake up!" she heard him say, a soft laugh behind the words. "We're here!"

She started, almost as if she actually had fallen asleep, and looked bewilderedly about. "Where? Where are we?"

"This is where I live."

The next moment he had alighted and was beneath her, holding forth his arms. She slid into them. He set her quickly onto the ground and began giving orders to the smartly uniformed lackeys who had appeared with almost magical promptness.

While he was occupied with them, Jacintha looked about.

They were at the entrance of what appeared to be an enormous mountain lodge or hotel—so tremendous that it certainly could house whoever had been sent here from the beginning of sin to the present.

The building was made of dark, rough, weather-stained logs. It had great spreading porches and innumerable shining windows. Boxes filled with bright flowers stood along the porch walls, hung from overhead and attached beneath every window. Elk- and deer-horns projected high above the doors and at intervals along the veranda. Totem poles, blue and red and yellow, stood on either side of the doorway. The building was a very fine one, handsome to look at, well planned and executed. Its only peculiarity, so far as she could see, was that it was not yet finished. Various wings jutted out within her vision, and each was incomplete, a framework upon which workmen still labored.

Very likely he never would finish it, since new tenants were always turning up.

Having given several instructions, he turned, touched her elbow with one hand, and led her into the lodge. More lackeys followed them, and Jacintha was disgusted by the extreme degree of their humbleness, their cringing, sniveling desire to please the master. It seemed to annoy him, too, for he spoke to them rudely and, occasionally, gave one a kick that sent him sprawling.

The lobby was of such immensity that she could not

see from one end to the other. It, too, was finished with
crudely sawn logs. The ceiling must have been eighty feet
high, with tiers of balconies running around all sides.
Kerosene lamps dangled from varying heights. Shaggy
black and brown bear hides were hung on the walls and
flung across balcony railings. She could see one fireplace,
big enough to burn a twenty-foot log, and there must have
been several others to warm a hall of such stupendous
magnitude.

Furthermore, it was crowded.

Jacintha gazed about in wondering awe. If she had
found him impressive before, standing alone on Roaring
Mountain, to see him now in his own palace—which must
be what this was—surrounded by men and women who
were his subjects in every sense, made him soar suddenly,
in her estimation, to a glorious invincibility.

How little I am, she thought, with almost thankful
humbleness. And how great he is.

The next moment she was angry with herself for such
prideless servility and gave herself warning to be on guard
against his despotism, for his vigor threatened to lay waste
anything of lesser intensity.

She glanced about and saw that the men and women
who were strolling up and down, standing in groups of two
or three, talking, sitting in chairs along the walls or
examining articles apparently for sale in the small shops,
were all dressed in clothes of the latest fashion. Moreover,
their clothes were extraordinarily beautiful and looked very
expensive. She might have been at the Oriental Hotel in

Manhattan Beach—except, of course, that there were a number of Indians among them, half-naked like him, and painted with vermilion and yellow pigment and blue earth, or swathed in blankets. Some of the squaws, she saw to her horror, had had their noses cut off; she must find out why.

To the right, as they entered the hall, was a very long desk with a straggling line of men and women, apparently waiting for their accommodations to be assigned. Bellboys ran frantically up and down, laden with baggage, and what appeared to be at least an acre of trunks and suitcases stood in the center of the hall.

From time to time, as she waited, she discovered herself being stared at by various men to whom she gave a brief, cold look and haughtily turned her head. She was pleased to be standing at his side even if he was no longer paying attention to her, for he was engaged in a dozen conversations at once. His entrance had been a signal to the others, who came swarming—the women flirting, the men asking favors or telling him jokes. Sometimes he laughed. Other times he scowled and gestured the suppliant away. He looked magnificent.

And yet, they seemed an extraordinarily attractive group. It was a young-looking crowd, too. Few were beyond middle age and many were as young or younger than she: *Who said the good die young?*

At last, when she had waited a long while and he gave no sign of remembering her presence, talking above and around her to people on all sides, she grew impatient and angry. She touched his arm timidly, quickly withdrawing her fingers. He did not respond and gave no indication he had felt it.

She stepped up closer, put her hand on his forearm and lifted her voice to make it pierce the babble. "Please!"

He turned his head and glanced down, seemed puzzled for an instant, and then laughed. "Oh." He smiled. "I had forgotten about you." He snapped his fingers. "Boy!" A boy appeared instantly, scooting in among those who thronged about him, crouching slightly as if to dodge a blow. "Take this lady's baggage to Room 69000. Quick!" He did not speak to her or look at her again but, having given the order, turned instantly away and began to discuss buffalo hunting with two painted, naked braves.

Jacintha gave him a glance of hurt dismay, but the bellboy was already scuffling over to the baggage and she ran after him. He began searching for hers and seemed almost hysterical as he went crawling among the thousands of suitcases like a dog on a rabbit's scent. Jacintha strolled about to help him, and it was she who found them.

"Here!" she called. "Here they are!"

He gave her a quick, grateful, sheepish grin, came leaping and crawling, hastily shouldered the trunk, tucked one bag under his arm and picked up the other two. Then away he went. Jacintha was forced to run to keep up with him. They set off down a broad hallway. She followed as quickly as she could, but he was fast and cunning and at times he almost lost her.

Once he got two hundred feet or more away and she had to shout at him to wait. When she had almost caught up he went scuttling on again. Finally, panting, she came up behind him.

"Why are you in such a hurry?"

"I must get back. He may want me again."

"What if he does? What can he do to you? You're here now."

He gave her a roundabout glance and shuttled on. She took several more running steps. "You don't know him," he said, but refused to elaborate, though she coaxed him to tell her more.

It was incredible, how fast he went. He must have been doing this for years. A terrible thought entered her mind.

"How long have you been here?" she asked. It was not, of course, the length of his stay that interested her but the possible length of her own, to which she thought his answer might give a clue.

He kept hurrying ahead of her, the trunk across his shoulders and bent neck and head, the suitcases dangling from either arm. He seemed not to have heard.

"Please!" cried Jacintha, for now she was frightened. They kept rushing along those vast hallways and had taken so many turns that she would never be able to find her way back. She ran up beside him. "I'm new here, as you must know! Tell me something—answer my questions."

He glanced at her, and even as he did so, his own momentum carried him ahead once more. "Why must you bother me? Why can't you learn for yourself? Can't you see how busy I am?''

''You're not busy!'' she cried in anger and exasperation. ''Aren't you ashamed of yourself—rushing about as if you have no self-respect at all—terrified of that rascal out there?''

''Thank God! Here we are.''

He had stopped so suddenly that Jacintha almost ran past him, but brought herself up sharply before a closed door with brass numerals on it: Room 69000.

In a moment the door was open, and he grovelingly invited her to enter. She sailed into her new quarters and began to look them over appraisingly, while he unloaded her baggage, set a match to the wood in the fireplace, asked if there was anything else he could do and, when she shook her head, was out the door.

She ran after him, calling, ''Wait! I want to give you something.''

''Nothing, madam, thank you. The management won't permit it.'' He bowed low. He was already several yards away.

Jacintha surveyed him with contempt. ''You disgust me. God knows what *your* sin must have been.''

He bowed once more and, as he left, finally gave her a bit of information. ''We were the cowards and hypocrites. He hates us worse than anything.'' With that, he was off again.

Jacintha watched a moment as he went bowling along the hallway; he was so entirely repulsive.

At least, she reflected, as she turned and slowly closed the door—at least, I am not here for either of those sins. She felt somewhat pleased, almost smug, that her own vice had been, instead, the result of daring and recklessness.

I am here because—once I fell in love with Brian—I was honest enough to act, rather than be cowardly or hypocritical. Brian was everything in the world to me— He was my . . . She paused, uncertainly, then stopped, closed her eyes, and covered her face with her hands, trying to remember what Brian had looked like. She shut her eyes hard, trying intensely and with mounting anxiety, to recall his image.

Why can't I remember?

She flung out her arms in a sudden frantic despairing gesture and stared around the room, seeing nothing.

What has happened? I could always see him as clearly as if he were in the room. . . .

"In a couple of weeks, or less, you'll be so taken up with what's going on here that you will scarcely remember your former life. All the people you knew then will seem vague and unreal, as if you had only imagined them." So he had said.

Was that happening to her so soon? Was she forgetting Brian, for whom she had died? The thought was incredible, sickening, terrifying. She must put her mind on other things—her quarters here, which she had not yet investigated.

The room was large—luxurious and impressive. As she stood near the door she faced two ceiling-high windows hung with fresh gold-stamped muslin curtains and extravagantly looped draperies of crimson damask. Between the windows stood a small tulipwood desk, elegantly carved and inlaid with mother-of-pearl.

The walls were covered with crimson flocked paper, the texture of cut velvet. The Brussels carpet, reaching from wall to wall, had a flamboyant blue and red floral pattern. The white marble mantelpiece was surmounted by a great gold-framed mirror, opposite which stood the bed with its carved ebony headboard six feet tall and its spread of pale-blue velvet edged with heavy black fringe.

There were wax flowers under a glass dome on a marble-topped table. There were thickly upholstered blue velvet chairs with lavish swags and cascades of fringe; many lamps edged with sparkling crystal beads stood on elaborate tables.

The room was designed and furnished in the most perfect rococo taste. She would have been pleased to have such a room in her own home and, in fact, had had several which were not very different. Its only fault was that, like a hotel room, it was entirely without the personal touches or warmth of an inhabitant.

Exploring further, she found large closets and an adjoining private bathroom with a tub almost big enough to swim in.

I like this, she thought. I could be very happy here. If it were any place but here, she added ruefully.

How easy it was to forget, momentarily at least, where she was and what had happened to her. How easy—and how treacherous.

Well, at least, if she was to be punished—though she

was beginning to think that was a superstition believed in by fools—still, if she was to be punished, it evidently would not consist in the deprivation of any material comforts. These surroundings were as rich and handsome as her own had been, and she even had with her many of her own clothes. Things could be very much worse.

Jacintha strolled to the window.

The sky was still bright blue and the clouds foaming white, as if they had been stirred by a swizzle stick. Before her window in a great sweep lay a desolate scene of bare earth on which nothing stood erect but dead trees and yellow goldenrod. To one side was a boiling hot lake and in its center spouted a geyser, spraying and splashing from an apparent excess of energy. Steam coming from it whirled like a dancer, then drifted in slow, desultory fashion, obscuring and revealing the landscape, behaving as if it were a coquettish woman with a scarf or veil. Far in the distance, halfway up a pine-covered mountain, steam shot upward in a great cloud so that it appeared as if the mountain had blown open and was spending itself in ecstasy, or in anger.

His handiwork was awe inspiring and discomforting, too. It was not so easy to forget where she was.

She turned abruptly. *I'll unpack. That will take my mind off thinking for a while.*

Her dress was dusty and wrinkled from the long trip, and she got out of it, a feat not very easy to accomplish alone. She slipped on a dressing gown of sheer white nainsook with pink satin ribbons laced through it, a four-foot ruffled train that dragged about the room and pink roses tacked here and there upon the skirt. In this becoming costume she stepped before the tall mirror over the dressing table and moved slowly through a personal ballet that had produced, in private, some of her most effective public gestures.

She smiled and her face was suddenly radiant. She lifted her chin and gazed at herself from half-closed eyes. She turned and cast a quick winsome glance across her shoulder. She swept forward, gracious, serene, and proud. Her body seemed to melt with delicate seductiveness from one attitude to the next.

But though, in her previous life, she had been beautiful for herself as much as for anyone—even Brian—now she was interested only in what *his* response to her beauty would be. What expression, what look or tone or mannerism would please him most? She must try to remember when it was he had looked at her with the greatest interest, exactly how she had been standing and what she had been doing at that moment. And, next time she saw him, she must notice very carefully what pleased him and what he was indifferent to.

Then she paused, leaned forward, and looked at herself long and carefully.

What has he done to you?

You were so scornful of that lackey. What about your own pride? He will despise you, for sure, if he sees you so eager for approval.

She turned away.

41

Something must be terribly wrong with me. I don't even know him—and everything that I know about him is bad. He's the wickedest man who ever lived, so wicked that even God could not forgive him. And I stand here wondering how I can please him!

She turned, went swiftly to her trunk and began to take things out of it, laying her gowns on chairs and across the bed, tossing her shoes into a heap on the floor, piling her fans and pincushions on a tabletop. She was so helpless, so untrained to do anything for herself, even to unpack a trunk and put her clothing away. The more things she unpacked, the more disordered and littered and confused the room got and the greater was her own distraction and anxiety: *I'll never get this done!*

Never? Well, I have forever!

And suddenly, for the first time, she felt a dreadful, empty loneliness and despair. *Once these things are put away—what is there for me to do?* She began to turn, glancing around the room. There were no books, and none had been included in her luggage. There was no needlework. There was no harp. There were no paints or sketchbooks. She could not talk to the cook or visit her friends or have a new gown fitted or drive in Central Park or play with the children or steal out to meet Brian or plan her next dinner party or accompany her husband to the theater or opera. She could not do anything—but wait, and hope that he would send for her.

Frantically, her face drained white, her dark eyes big with terror, she began to dart about the room, lifting covers, shoving chairs aside, peering into corners, bending down to look under the bed. She had no idea what she was looking for, but her search became increasingly wild and excited.

There must be something for me to do!

She was on her knees, surrounded by all the disarray of her garments and belongings, when she was surprised by a light rap at the door.

She rose instantly, afraid that she would be discovered in this hysterical, undignified attitude.

"Come in!" she called.

After a brief silence, the knob turned slowly, the door was pushed gently open, and there stood a very beautiful young woman, smiling at her. "May I come in?" she asked, in a tone that was at once sweet, clear, and compelling.

"Yes. Please do." Tremendously relieved at the appearance of a visitor, Jacintha moved forward, wondering what she wanted and why she had come.

"I wonder," said Jacintha's visitor, "if I might ask you to hook me up the back. It's my maid's afternoon off and I can't reach them myself."

"I'd be glad to," said Jacintha with eager graciousness. The room felt warmer and friendlier to her already. Some of her terror was dissipating.

The woman turned and Jacintha began to hook up her dress. It was an evening gown of rich, heavy black satin and fitted almost to her knees, as though it had been plastered onto her corset. The skirt, in front, was an intricate arrangement of diagonal folds, finished with two rows of pleated white ruffles. In back it had a five-foot train and was hung with masses of velvet loops caught by clusters of wisteria blossoms. The bodice was cut low and square to show superbly shaped arms and shoulders and the full beginning rise of lovely breasts.

"What a beautiful gown!" cried Jacintha. It was one she would have enjoyed wearing herself.

She finished the last hook and her visitor turned, smiling, touching the back of her hair with delicate fingers. "Thank you. I think it is, too." She revolved slowly so that Jacintha could admire it from all angles, for a fashionable gown was meant to create a different portrait of its wearer at every turn of the body.

The young woman was perhaps two or three inches shorter than Jacintha and seemed to have a somewhat more voluptuous figure. Her hair was a rich red-brown, drawn back off her ears, with a mass of curls upon her forehead, while in back it fell into a luxuriant cascade of folds and twists and braids. Her eyes were dark, large, soft, and brilliant, with long lashes.

Her manner was eager and artless; her beauty so vivid and ripe that she seemed almost literally to bewitch her surroundings.

She and Jacintha stood silently a moment and looked at each other, smiling with honest friendship. Perhaps because they were essentially different kinds of women, they could admire each other objectively, each taking pleasure in the other's beauty. Since beautiful women live a life very different from that of unfavored ones, they were drawn together and felt a common bond.

"Won't you sit down?" asked Jacintha. "I just arrived, as you can see—" She gestured at her open trunk and bags and the welter of gowns and petticoats, gloves and fans, lying everywhere. She swept a heap of garments off one of the chairs and offered it to her guest.

"Thank you." The young woman smiled and seated herself delicately and gracefully, crossing her narrow, pointed black satin slippers. "I may as well tell you the truth. My maid *was* there. But I had to have some excuse to come and visit. You don't mind, do you? It's lonely here. There are so many people and so much excitement, yet one is always lonely. Perhaps it's the lack of a goal, or perhaps it's just knowing that it's forever. . . ."

Jacintha watched her as she talked, speaking with such sweetness and gaiety, without any complaint in her tone, yet with an intense pathos. She listened as though she were herself a casual visitor, having no part in the afflictions of the permanent residents—until all at once she realized that this was her predicament, too. A chill went down her arms and back, ending in an uncontrollable shudder.

Her visitor chatted on lightly. "The millennia go fast enough, I'm told. It's the moments that drag."

Jacintha swallowed. Her throat felt dry, and her breath was coming quickly but with difficulty. She wanted to ask how long her new friend had been here, but it seemed such a tactless question. Worse than tactless— cruel, as well.

The other woman was looking at Jacintha, her head

tilted to one side, slightly smiling. "You are here," she said, "because you committed adultery. Your husband was jealous and he killed you."

Jacintha's hand went to her face, which had turned white, and she took a step backward. "How did you know that?" she whispered.

The other woman stood and came close to Jacintha, touching her hand with warm, tender fingers. "I'm sorry if I startled you. I simply felt it, that's all. It's the very reason that I am here—though my husband did not shoot me. He was subtle. He used poison and people thought I had died of consumption. The moment I entered the room I sensed it."

"You did?" asked Jacintha, wonderingly. "Isn't that strange?"

"Everything is strange here, although seemingly commonplace. Look at me. You probably want to know how long I've been here. . . . It's been twenty years."

"But—you—"

"I know. I haven't changed at all. Neither will you. That's one consolation—you'll never get any older than you are today. Age is the penalty you pay for staying alive." She made a little gesture, shrugging slightly, and smiling. Every move she made, every inflection of her voice, was both spirited and oddly touching at the same time.

"Well," said Jacintha, "at least that is something."

"There are other things, too," said the visitor softly.

Jacintha waited for her to continue, but the woman

did not elaborate. Instead, she opened a beaded jet bag and took out an enameled fan-shaped mirror into which she glanced for a moment, touching a curly tendril beside her cheek, musing pleasantly to herself. Then she slipped the mirror back into the bag, glanced at Jacintha, and smiled.

"Are you sorry?" she asked, after a moment. "Do you wish you had been cautious and respectable and... cowardly?"

Jacintha frowned, catching her lower lip with her teeth, and looked down at the roses in the richly patterned carpet. She put one forefinger beside her mouth and thought carefully of what her visitor had asked. Finally she raised her head and they faced each other directly.

"No," she said. "Once I met Brian, everything else had to follow. I know it was wicked, at least according to the world, but it wasn't wicked to me—or, if it was, I preferred it to being moral. My life, I suppose, was quite gaudy—not at all suited to the times in which I lived." This last she added with just a touch of pride.

The other sighed and lightly tapped her fan against the palm of her hand. "Yes—that's a lesson which seems very difficult for women like us to learn. Whatever age you live in, you must live up to it and accept it, or you are damned. Perhaps because we are beautiful, we have so very much more temptation. It's so easy, haven't you noticed, for plain women to condemn beautiful ones?"

They smiled at each other, like two gently mannered conspirators.

"And yet," added Jacintha after a moment, "I had dignity. I was never coarse or common. My mother would not have been ashamed of me—if she had lived."

"I am *sure* she would not," said the other woman warmly, and reached out impulsively to touch her arm. "Come—let's be friends. We are already. Heavens—" She gave a light, pretty gesture of mild distraction— "I haven't even introduced myself. My name is Charity, though I have always been called Cherry. Cherry Anson."

"My name," Jacintha said quietly, after a trembling moment, "is Jacintha Anson Frost."

The other woman drew in her breath sharply. "Why—then—you are my child!" Her eyes grew faintly sorrowful as she looked at Jacintha's face. "You died so young?"

Jacintha inclined her head. "The same age you were, Mother. Isn't it strange?"

Cherry was still watching her, very carefully, with great interest and appraisal. "I wonder." She sighed a little and held out her arms.

Jacintha hesitated a moment and suddenly, with the same throat-tearing, agonizing love she had felt when she was five years old, knowing in some fathomless way that her mother was dying and would never hold her in her arms again, they stood together, close and silent, until Jacintha began to cry.

"No, my darling." said Cherry softly, coaxingly. "No. There's nothing to cry about. I was sorry to leave you, but I was not sorry to die. I don't believe anyone is, really. Do you?"

She stood back, her hands still holding Jacintha's shoulders, and Jacintha faced her, tears streaming down her cheeks, little sobs breaking from her spasmodically. She had not felt her mother's death with this tormenting keenness since the day she had watched the coffin being lowered into the ground. Then she had begun to wail uncontrollably so that her father had picked her up and held her, trying to comfort her. The sobbing had continued for two or three days, until she was sick and exhausted.

Until this moment, her mother had been a sweet and cherished memory.

"*He* killed you!" cried Jacintha, her voice strangling and harsh. "He poisoned you!" She gave a long moan and, covering her face with her hands, sank to her knees.

Cherry knelt swiftly beside her, putting her arms about her, stroking her hair, as if she were, indeed, that five-year-old child she had last known her daughter to be.

"Don't cry, Jacintha. Don't cry, please. Here we are—together, after all. Why, it's as if a miracle had happened, that we even found each other here. Look, Jacintha—look at me—" She was smiling eagerly, though once or twice she had to brush a tear from her own cheek and give her head a quick, admonishing shake. She put her hand beneath Jacintha's chin and gently turned her face upward. "Look what's happened to us. Here we are—together—and both of us at the very best time of our lives!"

"The very best time of our lives," repeated Jacintha. "Except that we're dead."

The two women looked at each other, then suddenly

started to laugh. They laughed as if at the greatest joke they had ever heard, rocking backward and forward, their voices pealing out, rippling one over the other like bells struck in different steeples, laughing and laughing and laughing, until they had to fold their hands across their stomachs and bend double with the pain of it.

"Oh!" they gasped every few moments. "Oh!"

Gradually their laughter subsided and they sat, still facing each other, sober and solemn now, every trace of merriment gone.

"What a terrible thing it is," said Jacintha. "You . . . and me. We should have lived a long, long time. We had every right to life and happiness and love! We're the kind of women who should not have died until . . ."

"Until we were old?" asked Cherry softly. "And had lost our beauty and grown bitter on the memories of it? I've thought about this a great deal, Jacintha. It's not a game that can be won by anyone, no matter how clever or how lucky. What do you suppose would have happened to you and Brian if you had lived?"

"We'd have gone on, of course, as we were. Being happy."

"You loved him?"

"I did. I loved him completely—as he loved me. I loved him the way—" She hesitated, searching for an expression.

"I know," said Cherry, and bowed her head. "The way I loved the man your father killed me for. But there's something more, Jacintha, which may not have occurred to you. It's this: In any perfect love there is a finality which is terrifying—because it is deathlike. A love of that kind is very rare, of course, but when it happens, I think then it is time to die.''

Jacintha shook her head. "Oh. I *can't* believe that! I don't know what I think or believe—but not that. Love is the purpose and end of life!''

"Yes," agreed Cherry gently. "The end of life. When women die as we did, still young and beautiful and very much loved, don't you think it's more suitable to us than if we had waited too long? We died the way a story should end—at its climax.''

Cherry rose gracefully to her feet and stood smoothing the folds of her gown, then she walked to the mirror and touched the sides and back of her hair, holding up a hand mirror and turning this way and that.

Momentarily forgetting her own beauty, Jacintha watched her mother with tender admiration, then went to stand beside her.

"Your hair looks so beautiful. That's *such* a becoming style. Would you show me how to do mine like it?'' She sounded wistful and appealing, like a little girl, and Cherry turned to her with a quick, impulsive smile.

"Of course I will. It would look wonderful on you. It's the newest thing, you know.''

"I'm sure it is. Oh, Mother—'' She had begun with a rush of eagerness but, at that word, she stopped and frowned, a puzzled look on her face, and regarded them both in the mirror. "That sounds odd. I don't believe I can call you that—under the circumstances. May I call you—"

"Of course, darling. Call me by my name."

"Cherry. Such a lovely name. At our home in the country I had Martin plant cherry trees. And every spring, when they bloomed, I would go out and bring in branches of them. I loved them more than any other flower." She bowed her head again, and shut her eyes. "How I missed you!"

"Hush, darling." Cherry touched her cheek. "Don't cry anymore. Why—it seems more like Heaven than Hell. And we're together now—for eternity."

"Yes. For eternity," repeated Jacintha, gazing across her mother's shoulder, out the great window. "Though I still have not the vaguest comprehension of it."

"They say you never do," said Cherry softly. "I've talked to people who've been here two, three...five thousand years! They all say exactly what you did. I believe it's best not to think about it," she finished crisply. "Now darling, why don't you get dressed and we'll have a stroll in the lobby, talk to some people, and then it'll be time for dinner."

"Yes. Let's do that." She walked to her trunk and then turned back once more. "Will you stay with me?"

"Of course I will. May I help?"

"No, thank you. I don't want you to help. I want you to sit and talk to me. You say they serve dinner? Things aren't so very different in the essentials, are they?"

"In the essentials—they are. For, while they serve

everything, wonderful food, too, you don't need it to sustain life, and consequently you don't enjoy it."

"Then why does anyone bother?"

"It's something to do. As I think of it, I don't believe I've been to dinner in a year or two—possibly longer."

"Really?" cried Jacintha. "Isn't that incredible!" She sounded almost pleased at this odd and interesting bit of information.

They continued chatting merrily, like two schoolgirls spending the night together, exchanging confidences, asking opinions and advice, going over all the minute details of their lives and deaths.

While Jacintha moved about, hanging her gowns in the closet, setting her shoes in neat rows, arraying her hats along the top shelves, folding her dainty, lace-trimmed petticoats and chemises, Cherry lounged on a sofa, playing with her fan. The sofa was curved up high at one end and dwindled to nothing at the other; it was covered with crimson velvet and made a strikingly effective background for her black satin gown and cream-colored skin. As the afternoon faded, Jacintha lighted the kerosene lamps which, reflecting off the crimson walls, filled the room with a delicate, intimate rose-tinted glow.

"I always knew your father would be sorry that he killed me," said Cherry. "And I'm glad to hear that he was."

"I don't believe he had one happy moment after you died. Of course, we all thought it was because he had loved you so much. He visited the cemetery every Sunday with armloads of flowers. When the weather was nice, we spent the entire afternoon. Your grave was very beautiful—there was a fringed marble cushion on top and an inverted torch. We would sit under the weeping willow he planted the day of your funeral, and he would stare at the stone and sigh. Your stone was very tenderly engraved, too, with a verse he composed himself. It read..."

Cherry, who had listened to this recital with a look of contemptuous amusement, now quickly raised her hand. "Please. I couldn't bear hearing it. Tell me, were you and your father close?"

"No. I never liked him. I don't quite know why, but I was afraid of him after you died. He was kind to me—almost too kind, out of his own guilty feelings, I suppose." She paused, holding in her arms several bonnets covered with flowers and ribbons and feathers. "And yet, in a way, I was fascinated by him."

Cherry laughed again, her happy, rippling laugh, which sounded to Jacintha like a long-delayed echo, reaching her twenty years after it had first been scattered into the air.

"A man can generally be fascinating as a father even if he was never successfully fascinating as a husband. It's the greatest comfort most of them have, poor dears."

"Oh!" cried Jacintha delightedly. "How witty you are! How wonderful it is to be with you again!"

"Aren't we fortunate? What are you going to wear tonight?" They strolled into the closet, Jacintha holding a kerosene lamp in one hand, and began to look through her wardrobe. "You must wear your most beautiful gown. He may be there and, if he is, I want you to make a good first impression."

Jacintha turned with a look of surprise. In all their eagerness to get reacquainted, she had not thought to mention her encounter with him. "But I've already made my first impression!"

"What? You've met him? Already? Where?"

"Why, I met him on Roaring Mountain by Lemonade Lake." The tentative sound of her voice, vague and soft and wondering, indicated that now she was doubtful. "This place," she said, and brushed one hand before her face. "It's like living in a mirage, isn't it?"

Cherry had been watching her carefully, her expression showing concern—and something more, a kind of hurt dismay, as well. "How did it happen?" asked Cherry finally, and then she gave a self-conscious little laugh. "Both of you on Roaring Mountain. That's a strange place for a meeting."

"His coachman—Grant, he called him—made me get out there. I didn't want to, but he insisted. And there he was—the . . . the Devil, I mean. What a start he gave me! I turned around, not thinking there was a soul within miles and saw him standing there, looking at me. When I screamed, he laughed."

As she was speaking, the feeling he had roused in her returned, to rush through her body like the sudden flight of startled birds, leaving her stunned and bewildered. She experienced once more the profound shock of his fierce and dazzling beauty. She grew warm and restless, filled with the memory of his vast, menacing energy and vigor. Undoubtedly, he had enthralled her, without gallantry or flattery or any kind of obeisance. And that, in itself, was a frightening realization.

She glanced at Cherry, and they looked at each other for a long moment; Jacintha's face clearly puzzled and unhappy, Cherry's surprised, chagrined, but solicitous, as well. Quickly, briefly, she patted Jacintha's hand.

"He loves to do that," said Cherry reassuringly. "He loves to scare people, you know. Girls especially." She turned then and started slowly out of the closet. "He must have been eager to meet you."

"Don't go!" cried Jacintha. "We haven't selected my gown."

Cherry swung back, laughing, tilting her head so that the clear line of her throat and chin was displayed, and her laugh had a sound that made Jacintha think of coins flung into the air, tinkling together as they fell. "Of course! What was I dreaming of? Sometimes I'm featherbrained, darling. Forgive me." She touched Jacintha's arm and clasped it for a moment, smiling directly into her face. Her charm and warmth and beauty were so great, Jacintha marveled that she had ever arrived in Hell. Surely she could have softened the heart of any villain, even her father.

"Do you know," said Jacintha softly, "you're the first beautiful woman I've ever known that I wasn't furiously jealous of—deep down, that is."

"I know. I feel the same. I'm delighted to find you have grown into such a beauty . . . but I knew you would. You were the loveliest child anyone ever saw. That's why we're not jealous of each other, I suppose. Being mother and daughter, our beauty seems a mutual possession— yours belongs to me and mine to you, and we admire it in each other as we admire it in ourselves. It's a very comforting and rather mystical kind of love, isn't it?"

"This has been the happiest day of my life," avowed Jacintha, and they both laughed. "Now—what shall I wear? You really think he'll be there?"

"Do you hope he will?" Cherry asked. "Are you looking forward to seeing him again?"

Jacintha frowned. "I suppose I am. After all, he's the only man of any consequence around here."

"How did he strike you?"

At that question, her confusion grew almost tumultuous; she turned her back and pretended to be looking through her dresses. She would have been ashamed for her mother to know how much he had impressed her.

"Why—" she said, after a few seconds— "he's rather attractive, I suppose—in a crude sort of way. Certainly, he's no gentleman." Of all the absurd things to say!

"No," agreed Cherry, "he is not. Here—why don't you wear this one? I think it's charming."

Jacintha frowned. "It's very pretty, but—isn't it rather dull?" she asked anxiously. It was the gown her husband had liked to see her wear when he entertained his most conservative friends.

"Oh, yes," agreed Cherry, musingly. "It is a little dull. Well, then, wear this one. I'm sure you'll create a great sensation in it. And you may as well, after all."

The gown Cherry held up now was one Jacintha had bought the summer before when she and Martin were in Paris; it was made of velvet in the very fashionable solferino: a vivid purple-pink. Color could not be too rash or clamorous for high fashion. It was, in fact, the gown she had worn to the ball where she had met Brian. But she felt shy about mentioning that now, for fear Cherry might think she was hoping to cast the same spell tonight. For, of course, she was.

It took an hour and a half for Jacintha to bathe, arrange her hair—with Cherry's help—and get dressed. All the while, they continued talking.

Jacintha wanted to find out if Cherry knew him or what kind of man he was, but when she asked, Cherry only said, "Yes, I know him. At least, I've spent quite a bit of time in his company, which is all anyone can say about knowing him. People never agree about him. He seems one kind of man to one person and quite different to another. So you see, anything I might tell you would never match your own opinions. Wait and decide for yourself. Now, let's not talk about him anymore. He's a disturbing subject, at best, which is what he wants to be, of course. Let me warn you of only one thing. Don't be misled by his good looks or any charm he may choose to show from time to time. He's not the Devil for nothing, you know."

Jacintha listened carefully and soberly, like a little girl receiving her first lesson in school, nodding her head from time to time. "I think there was something . . . sinister about him."

Cherry sighed heavily and brushed at the air with her spangled black chiffon fan. "He's all things to all men and women. Please, Jacintha, let's not discuss him anymore."

"No. We won't. I'm sorry I ever brought him up. Tell me what people do here for amusement."

"Well, let me see," began Cherry slowly. Now she was drawing on her long white kid gloves and buttoning them at the wrists. "There is a great deal of gambling, for instance."

"Gambling!" Jacintha stood before her dressing table, sorting among her jewels. "Is that the best way they can find to waste their time?"

Cherry shrugged delicately. "Yes. It's one of the best. He invented it, you know. Then there is . . ."

"Look what I have here!" cried Jacintha. She was standing before Cherry holding a wide, lacy necklace and bracelet with heavy gold fastenings, made of Cherry's own red-brown hair. "All my life Father wore a watch chain made of your hair."

Cherry stared with polite curiosity for a moment, one hand absentmindedly patting her hair. "How dismal. I had one, too, you know, of my mother's hair. We *were* morbid, weren't we?"

Jacintha looked at her treasures with disappointment. Cherry, it seemed, had lost many of her values since coming to this place. Sadly, she returned the baubles to her jewel case and they talked, instead, about Jacintha's collection of blue china.

At last she was ready. Her face was discreetly powdered and rouged, her hair plaited, twisted, and scrolled, with a cluster of three pale-blue ostrich tips at one side of her elaborate coiffure. Her white kid gloves were buttoned to the elbows, and she carried a small fan of matching pale-blue ostrich feathers. In her ears were single diamond studs; over her left breast, artfully arranged, a pair of diamond-encrusted stars; and circling her throat was a diamond necklace that had been Martin's last present to her.

Cherry and Jacintha complimented each other with warm enthusiasm and sincerity as they set out down the broad, deserted gaslit hallway.

Cherry, in her black satin gown, was small, soft, quick, and vivacious; Jacintha, in purple-pink velvet, was somewhat taller, lustrous, and tranquil. They strolled arm in arm, passing one closed door after another, their trains sweeping behind them, their murmuring voices fading in the vast, dim silence.

Out here, it was cold and empty, and they appeared as diminutive figures moving along the endless corridors. They chatted and laughed softly, sounding as happy and carefree as two young girls on their way to an eagerly anticipated ball.

Drifting along, traversing one passageway, turning the corner only to confront another, moving down that one and, by degrees, progressing through the maze of galleries along which Jacintha had earlier followed the scuttling lackey, they did not encounter another soul. When it seemed they had been walking forever, Jacintha turned to Cherry.

"Are we lost?"

"Oh, no. Don't be frightened. I know the way— we'll get there. This is a big place, you know. And he keeps adding to it all the time. He's constantly building. Nothing ever satisfies him. Well, we don't care about that, do we?"

Both women laughed.

In turn, each one gesturing with a delicate, round arm, Jacintha flirting out her feathered fan, Cherry sweeping her spangled black one, they moved their pointed shoes in easy, continuous patterns, pink velvet toes and black satin toes emerging and retreating.

Jacintha felt as if she were in a mild but delicious state of delirium, intoxicated, as it were, by some inner happiness, greater by far than any she had previously experienced. "I can't imagine what's happened to me," she confided. "I feel drunk."

She felt reckless, in fact, and that was not her nature. Though she had done reckless things, she was not of such a temperament. And the recklessness made her feel as if she were going somewhere in a great hurry, somewhere she had not chosen or planned to go, but to which she was nevertheless hastening with almost preternatural speed.

"One has to get acclimatized to any new place, you know," said Cherry, as if to minimize this high-spirited excitement which had taken hold of Jacintha.

For the past several minutes there had been a murmuring sound, low and indefinite, floating all around them. Now, suddenly, it escalated to a hideous, rumbling roar; a noise of great physical force that came rolling at them.

"Good heavens!" cried Jacintha. "What is that?"

"The lobby. It's around this corner. It's always frightfully crowded at this hour. Everyone comes before dinner to see and be seen, to gossip and flirt and find out what the others are doing."

They turned the corner and came to a set of double doors above which the motto WELCOME had been worked in branches garnished with clusters of pinecones. The doors were opened for them by two lackeys.

Cherry and Jacintha swept majestically through, heads high, fans unfurled, arms held gracefully so as not to obscure the contours of their bodies—two women accustomed to commanding instant attention and admiration.

The lobby was now packed full from one end to the other—a mass of people standing elbow to elbow, toe to toe, face to face, back to back, all in evening clothes—a dazzle of white shoulders and bosoms, diamonds glittering at ears and throats, aigrette and ostrich plumes waving, and elaborate fitted gowns displaying tiny waists between swelling breasts and hips. The room burst with brilliant color—royal blue, garnet, purple, scarlet, emerald green. The fabrics were rich—satins, velvets, taffetas, laces, tulles, heavy with bead and jet embroidery. They were ornamented, as well, by every conceivable arrangement of folds and frills, bows and tassels and ribbons and knotted

fringe. Their elegance and splendor were almost stupefying. The men wore elegantly tailored black-and-white
dinner dress.

An incessant babble was carried on in high-pitched
feminine tones and deep masculine voices, and the room
split and crackled with laughter, as though lightning
played through the atmosphere above their heads. Jacintha had never heard a group so excited, so amused by its
own conversation, so entirely given to pleasure and hi-
larity.

"Oh," she moaned, and one hand rose involuntarily
to touch her throat. "How dreadful the noise is!"

Their jabbering, in fact, was so piercing, it battered so
hard at the walls and smashed so violently at the ceiling,
that there seemed an almost literal danger it might blow
the building apart.

"It's always like this in the evening. I hate it. But
you'll get used to it in time. I think they create the noise to
keep themselves from thinking. They're all bored to
death."

"The confusion . . ."

"Let's stand here a moment. Look around, Jacintha,
and take stock of things, since this is where you'll be from
now on."

"Oh, I'm not so sure," she said doubtfully. Her
exhilaration was gone. "I may not care for it."

"You'll get used to it."

Jacintha turned, lifting her shiny black brows. "And
even if I don't, I can't leave, can I?"

Cherry slowly turned her head, and they looked at

each other briefly. Cherry's eyes swept over Jacintha's face, and at last she smiled, a rather subtle smile of tolerant amusement. "Of course not," she said finally. "That's the—"

"That's the hell of it!"

And gleefully Jacintha threw back her head and burst into laughter. But then, just as suddenly, she sobered, clapped her white-gloved hand to her mouth and stared, her eyes opened wide.

"You didn't really believe it, did you?" asked Cherry gently.

"No." Jacintha bowed her head, looking down at the toes of her pink velvet shoes. "I believe I thought I was on a visit."

"Well! So here you both are!"

It was a man's voice, hearty and commanding, just behind them. The two women turned with a start, giving little involuntary shrieks of surprise. He stood smiling down at them.

He wore a double-breasted dinner coat with quilted black satin lapels, a soft, tucked white shirt and black silk tie. He was even more awesome than he had been earlier in the day, for the contrast between this conventional formal style of dress, no different from that worn by every other man present, was so irresistible that he seemed to blaze with a new savage glory.

"My, my," whispered Jacintha, transfixed.

How truly miraculous to see a man of such matchless and terrible beauty. The effect he produced was not merely the result of his being incomparably handsome; it was, far more, the monumental energy he seemed to possess, volcanic and inexorable.

How wicked he is.

How evil. How cruel. How destroying.

She was so completely lost, so victimized and intoxicated, that several seconds had passed before she realized that, after the first quick glance at her, he had been looking at Cherry.

His expression was appraising and proprietary, his eyes glancing up and down her body and across her face with a lewd boldness. Cherry had, indeed, as she had said, spent quite a bit of time in his company. And the time had not been occupied with polite talk or questions concerning her soul.

Now, all at once, Jacintha remembered a number of seemingly innocuous things: Cherry's expression when Jacintha had recounted their meeting on Roaring Mountain; Cherry's recommendation that she wear a simple and innocently styled gown; Cherry's refusal to discuss him and the trace of alarm she had shown at Jacintha's frank statement that he was the only man here worth taking into consideration.

It was all quite plain now: Cherry had felt that wretched twist of jealousy, familiar to every woman upon the merest hint that the man she desires may pay flattering attention to someone else.

Her mother, then, was in love with the Devil. She had been bewitched by him; nothing could be more obvious. The way she looked up at him, her beauty so intensified by eagerness and ardor that she had become almost iridescent—that much was bad enough, but it was not the worst. For Cherry's innocent, proud little face now immodestly betrayed a sensual and wanton longing.

Seeing it, Jacintha felt a disgust and abhorrence that made her skin crawl. It was almost unbelievable, yet it was undeniable. They were smiling into each other's eyes with a monstrous intimacy, detestable beyond anything Jacintha had ever witnessed. Frantically, she longed to spring between them, give them each a violent slap, and break apart their private, impure world. Never had she felt such loathing and revulsion.

She must do something!

At that instant her fan, which she had been furiously fluttering without being aware of it, dropped to the floor.

"Oh!" she cried, looking down helplessly.

It took a moment longer, but finally he looked down, too. Then he gazed up at Jacintha, and slowly he smiled. She felt her face grow hot. He made no move to retrieve the fan. Was he going to force *her* to stoop and pick it up?

She was overwhelmed with confusion, and her dismay soon reached an intolerable pitch. Just then, he caught the eye of one of his hovering lackeys, and the fan was whisked off the floor and returned to her by a cringing fellow who bowed so low she could not even see his face.

Jacintha took it, her lashes lowered to conceal her eyes. "Thank you. I'm sorry."

And making her predicament even more unendurable, she heard Cherry's pattering laugh and felt her arm go about her waist.

"Poor child. You've upset her."

Oh! thought Jacintha, frantically. I can't stand this! What is she trying to do to me?

Jacintha's head was bowed so low that it seemed as if a strong hand pressed hard upon the back of her neck, making it impossible for her to lift it even if she tried. She wanted to run out of the lobby and out of the building and far away. But she did not know where to go. She would get lost, and she was afraid of being captured by Indians or attacked by wild animals or even falling through the thin crust around the geysers and being boiled.

Cherry's voice sounded lilting and gay and her arm tugged coaxingly at Jacintha's waist. "Don't be shy, darling. He looks much worse than he is." Jacintha heard both of them laugh at this, as if it were a highly amusing joke.

But she was mortified by Cherry's buoyant and sprightly manner with him, the obvious result of deep intimacy and prolonged association. Jacintha felt that Cherry had been dishonest, had cheated her, in fact. For while she had earlier spoken of him with reservations amounting to actual resentment, now, in his presence, she was merry and frolicsome. She must have been referring to her relationship with him when she said that this place had "other compensations." Jacintha now recalled her mysterious refusal to be more explicit.

And here I am—dressed like this, trying to compete with her! And she knows it.

Jacintha flung back her head. The flush drained out

of her face leaving her skin white once more, fragile and clear; she stared at him directly, her large brown eyes full of sparkling hauteur and malice. She looked young and rather wild, like an animal challenged on its forest trail.

I'll never make that kind of fool of myself again.

She had the feeling that since he had said, "So here you both are!" an aeon or more had passed. It had been, of course, only a few seconds; even so, a profound and permanent change had occurred between her and Cherry. She felt a mournful nostalgia for that earlier and more innocent love they had lost—as one is constantly losing things on earth by the mere passage of time, altering continuously the balance within oneself and in relation to everyone else.

He was looking at Jacintha now and smiling. "Mother and daughter," he said softly, reflectively. "When one of you arrives, I know the other will be along."

"Are you always so presumptuous?" asked Jacintha.

Cherry gave her a look of surprise and then smiled proudly, as if pleased by her quick reply. He threw back his head and laughed. Then, all at once, he left them. He touched Jacintha lightly beneath the chin, smiled once more at Cherry, and was absorbed into the depths of the crowd. They turned to each other, eyes wide, lips pursed.

"Well!" they said.

"He's an odd one, isn't he?" inquired Jacintha, thinking it a good idea to minimize his effect.

Cherry laughed, but the sound was artificial, and

Jacintha heard her follow it with a tiny, soft sigh, of remorse or hopelessness. For a moment Cherry's lovely face seemed to droop and grow mournful. But then, almost before Jacintha could see it, she was smiling again and linking her arm through hers.

"Let's stroll around. I'll introduce you to a few people—if I see anyone I know."

"If you see anyone you know?" repeated Jacintha incredulously. "I should think you must know any number of people by now."

"Fewer than you might think. Look at this crowd— could you easily pick out a face you'd seen once before? There's no rhyme or reason to it, remember. This is the main lodge, but there are numbers of others, and often, just when you begin to get acquainted, and to like them, he transfers them somewhere else. There's no understanding anything he does."

"He's impossible," said Jacintha. She glanced at Cherry to see if that announcement would bring an expression of relief. It did not. Cherry frowned a little, as if it troubled her.

"He is, I suppose," she said, softly and slowly. "I've grown rather used to his ways during the past twenty years. I don't expect anything of him anymore—except what he gives."

"What he gives? What does he give? He looks to me as though he would never give anything."

"Let's not talk about it. I can't discuss him. He's not like anyone you've ever known." She stopped abruptly, turned and faced Jacintha. "You'll fall in love with him."

"*I'll* fall in love with him?"

"Perhaps you have already," said Cherry, and looked carefully into her daughter's face. "You won't be able to help yourself. Don't you see what mischief he is about now? We thought it was such a miracle, our finding each other as we did, the very day of your arrival. *He* did it. He put you in the room next to mine."

"But why? What does he hope for?"

Cherry drew a deep breath and stopped, closed her eyes briefly and then looked straight at Jacintha. "I love him, you see. No—you mustn't ask me why, or anything about it. When you love him, too, you will know. It will give him amusement to see what we do—what happens to us. Eternity is endless for him, too, Jacintha."

Slowly, as she listened, Jacintha's face had altered: shock, disbelief, repugnance showed in quick succession. Finally, there was defiance.

"That may be his plan, but he won't succeed."

"He never fails," said Cherry, with a sad and stricken little smile.

And seeing that look on her mother's face, Jacintha felt her heart break with tenderness and love. She swore that since Cherry had lost the power to rescue herself from this unruly passion, her own clear responsibility was to repudiate him entirely at this very moment. She clasped Cherry's hand in both her own.

"I promise you . . ." began Jacintha, with intense fervor and devotion.

"Please," whispered Cherry. The noise was so great that Jacintha could only see her lips move. "Promise me nothing. We're in no place for promises."

Then, with one of her swift, magical changes of mood that so surprised and delighted Jacintha, her face flashed into brightness and animation.

"Not another word!"

"Not another word," Jacintha agreed.

They were in the midst of the crowd now. The handsome, fashionably dressed men and women were talking inexorably into one another's faces, the women laughing and using their eyes and mouths as if determined to display their beauty to its utmost advantage, fluttering their fans, touching gloved hands to their hair, tapping one man's shoulder, now another's. They seemed, en masse, in a state of hysteria. The racket and din were clangorous; their expressions were intense and lively; their manner spirited to the point of desperation. Moreover, the room had grown much hotter since Cherry and Jacintha had arrived, and it felt as if the floor were sending up waves of stifling heat. The fans of the ladies beat faster and faster.

"They're all so eager." protested Jacintha. "Each one seems to be telling a story that's the most important story in the world."

"Practically all of them are talking to someone they've never seen before and will never see again. About the only time they ever do see each other is when they arrange an assignation."

"You mean, they talk a few minutes and then—
meet?"

"Why not?" asked Cherry reasonably.

"But doesn't it cause gossip?"

"They gossip, of course, but they don't censor."

"There's no need for secrecy or concealment?"

"Concealment from whom?"

"Why, from each other—from . . ."

Cherry smiled with affectionate reproval. "Come,
Jacintha. Remember where you are."

"Yes," agreed Jacintha, embarrassed. "I know. I
forget. And yet it's so much like the *real* places I have been
to." She was frowning, thinking over what Cherry had
said as they made their way in the crowd, a step every few
inches, then a pause, then another slight forward movement. "But that must take away a great deal of the
pleasure," she said, after a few moments.

"It does. It takes away most of it. At first, everyone is
nonplussed to think of being able to indulge themselves
limitlessly, with as many different lovers as they want and
as often as they want and no one to so much as lift an
eyebrow. But then, after a time, they find that it is
meaningless. They no longer enjoy their romances, and
soon they cease even to have them—except that now and
then, when a particularly attractive person turns up, they
grow hopeful. But the end is always the same—there is no
pleasure to speak of."

Jacintha had been listening with growing horror and,
at the last, she gave an uncontrollable shudder. "How
terrible! He's left everyone looking so beautiful, yet he's

taken away the delight of succumbing to temptation while
he himself remains the essence of temptation."

"Exactly," agreed Cherry. Her eyes took on a sly
slant, and she looked now like a mischievous, wily minx.
"Don't you agree he's extraordinarily clever? There are
people who believe that it is only sensual love that makes
being alive for fifty years or so endurable. How endurable
do you suppose eternity will be—without it?"

"Oh! How detestable! It would be better if he tor-
tured us."

"Isn't this torture? No, of course you don't know yet
whether it is or not."

"I don't believe it!" Jacintha violently declared. "I
won't believe it! There must be some way of finding
pleasure here."

"There is. And that is in his power, too."

"*What?*"

"Yes. You must have heard of that. He can give a
woman greater pleasure than she ever dreamed of. Now
come along, I'm going to introduce you to two men over
here. We've got to get our minds off him and onto
something else. If you concentrate too long on any one
thing it begins to make you a trifle daft, you know."
Jacintha marveled at how Cherry had managed to keep up
her spirits in this place that had begun to seem so vile and
hopeless.

She and Cherry were slowly maneuvering their way
through the throng. Now Cherry stopped with a little cry
of distraction and annoyance.

"Oh! Isn't that tiresome! They weren't the men I

thought they were. Don't you see how aggravating it is to have everyone dressed in the latest styles?'' she asked crossly. "It makes it absolutely impossible to find anyone you know. He says we love fashion, so he provides us with it. But he doesn't do it to please us. He does it the way he puts those mottoes over the door saying WELCOME and THOU, GOD, SEEST ME. He mimics our way of life—not from consideration for us, but from contempt.''

The noise seemed suddenly louder, as if a tidal wave of harsh, overpowering sound had broken over them. So violent and crushing was its force that they stood there, cringing inside, visibly wincing, both women feeling themselves bruised and wilted by the tremendous, booming roar. It rose around them, enveloped them, bore them down, pushed against them.

Cherry seemed close to tears. On every side they were being jostled, jolted, bumped against, and shoved.

"Shall we go back to our rooms?'' asked Jacintha tenderly.

Cherry brightened. "Yes, let's! Do you mind very much?''

"I want to. I can't wait to get out of here.''

Holding each other by the hand, Cherry steering, for she knew in which direction an exit might be found, they began the difficult, seemingly endless journey back. Cherry's spirits had noticeably revived and she talked quite gaily. Her eyes, glancing eagerly around, were obviously searching—the object of her search must be he.

His height would have given him away, but they

caught no glimpse of him. Perhaps he had gone into the gambling rooms, which were crowded at all hours with men and women agitated and engrossed like creatures obsessed, aware of nothing but the turning cards and rolling dice. Though they would neither lose nor win, they were hopelessly caught up in the sterile excitement.

Jacintha covertly watched as Cherry anxiously surveyed the gaming rooms. She must love him desperately to be so terribly afraid of having him see me again, she thought. Jacintha felt profound sorrow and despair; Cherry's shame seemed her own dishonor as well.

"You'll find you have very little in common," Cherry was blithely saying, "with people born in another age. You strike up a conversation with someone who looks interesting, and then find that he's a first-century martyr or a Renaissance priest. Pretty soon, you realize that it's almost impossible to find anyone of your own time and station, and you stop trying. He's the only one who seems to find something amusing about everybody."

Cherry kept saying that they must not talk about him anymore, but she also kept referring to him—unflatteringly, it was true, but so frequently that it was obvious he was constantly on her mind.

Jacintha intuitively sensed, from her own brief contact with him, that once a woman succumbed to the mesmeric force of his personality, she would then be at the mercy of a restless, vagrant nature, entirely given to its own caprice—pitiless, violent, arbitrary. She would have much to fear and almost nothing to hope for. And she would return, as if all the centuries of civilization had dissolved, to a defenseless servility, wholly in thrall to her own insatiable need. She would lose the dignity and aloofness, the power to refuse, which a woman must have for her own self-protection.

Jacintha found it more and more incredible that Cherry, dainty and sparkling, with her charming winsomeness, could be cast in this role of servitude. The realization made her sick, and a powerless fury began welling up inside her.

He's not the Devil for nothing, Cherry had said.

They arrived at the lobby doors without catching another glimpse of him; the lackeys flung them open and Cherry stepped aside, lightly touching Jacintha's back to usher her through. She glanced one last time over her shoulder, and the doors closed behind them.

Cherry was plainly relieved. She stood fanning herself, and Jacintha could see moisture on her forehead and little wisps of clinging hair. She sighed as if she had run a hard race, and then suddenly she laughed and lightly clapped her hands.

"We got out, didn't we? Every time I go in there I become terrified that I will never get out again!"

Jacintha felt a swelling burst of painful love, and she kissed her tenderly on the cheek.

Cherry shot her a glance of faint surprise, touched her finger to the spot, still tingling from Jacintha's kiss, and her eyes filled with tears.

Then, without either of them saying more, they

started back along the endless hallways.

When they finally reached Jacintha's room they couldn't wait to remove their tight-fitting gowns, laced corsets, and pointed shoes. Cherry dashed into her own room and was back in no time at all, wearing a graceful ruffled silk wrapper.

"I hated to leave you," she happily confided.

"I hated to have you leave."

But Jacintha knew that the real reason for Cherry's haste was her fear that if she left her daughter alone, he might appear.

I must find a way to make her feel safe about me. I must convince her somehow that nothing he could do could tempt me. I must give her back her self-respect. With other women she could bear it more easily; it is only with me that the jealousy must be intolerable.

Both women were now in their wrappers, loose and soft and flattering, billowed out by embroidered, ribbon-decorated petticoats. They talked to each other in the mirror as they stood with arms lifted high, removing pins and combs and feathers from their hair, tossing them onto the dressing-table top, which was a mass of cut-glass bottles and porcelain boxes filled with oils, scents, lotions, pomades; and pincushions, shaped like hearts and swans and guitars, covered with crystal beadwork and bristling with jeweled pins. The lamps were warmly burning, casting a soft and subtle light, and the heavy crimson draperies had been pulled together. A brisk fire was going in the fireplace, and the room seemed a cozy, intimate haven.

Surely, here they were safe from any intrusion. Indeed, it began to seem the threat to their companionship had been imaginary.

Had they ever been out in that wild, treacherous place?

Had they actually encountered and been forced violently apart by his explosive and ominous energy?

This was where they had been all along, softly talking, moving their hands and arms as gracefully as if they were performing a ballet, smiling in the mirror and admiring, with equal pleasure, their own selves and each other.

Both of them had luxuriant hair, falling down their backs below the waist—Jacintha's a shining black mass, waving and rippling and twisting into curls at the ends; Cherry's a deep, red-brown cascade. They had the same eyes, big and dark and splendidly radiant, and the same soft, pink mouths. They looked very much alike and, at the same time, very different. For while Cherry was sprightly and spontaneous, Jacintha, by contrast, had an unaffected pride and dignity which made her seem unintentionally imposing.

"Come," said Cherry. "Sit down and let me brush your hair, as I used to do. Remember? Such a very long time ago—"

Jacintha sat on a small violet-wood settee formed out of two gracefully curving chairs. Upholstered in crimson silk plush, roses and grapes were carved along the scalloped frames. Jacintha tilted back her head and Cherry, with slow, rhythmical strokes, began drawing the brush through her hair. For a few moments they were silent. Jacintha sat with closed eyes, trying not to cry; now that she and Cherry were together again, she felt a poignant nostalgia for those years that had been empty of her mother's gaiety and tenderness.

Unexpectedly, a sharp, spasmodic shudder began at her shoulders and traveled down her body. Then she laughed and gave Cherry a quick, apologetic little glance.

"Something just reminded me of Father. I guess I'm still a little afraid of him. Do you know he kept worrying that *I* would come down with consumption? He worried about it all my life, and I saw one doctor after another every time I caught a chill or ran a fever or even sneezed. I believe he finally convinced himself that you actually *had* died of consumption."

"Hypocrite!" said Cherry with sharp scorn. "I hope he doesn't die until he's very old. Imagine how boring that will make things for him here!" They both laughed, then Cherry said, "Let's make plans. Let's talk about all the things we're going to do together."

"Yes!" Jacintha clasped her hands in her lap like an eager child, sitting with her back very straight, her feet close together. "Let's make plans."

"This is the most picturesque country imaginable, you know. We can take a coach—a private one, or we can go in a public conveyance if we prefer—and travel about as much as we like. I haven't seen a great deal, for I simply never got around to it."

"Never got around to it! In twenty years?"

"The time went by so fast. It was gone before I knew it. I kept meaning to stir about—and then you arrived. We might even stay overnight and camp out. Don't you think that would be nice?"

"But it must be dangerous . . . bears and panthers and wild Indians. Wouldn't you be afraid?"

"I suppose. Well, then perhaps we can get together a party. Yes! That's what we'll do!"

They went on, talking and planning how they would fill sketchbooks with every wonderful sight they saw (as each had done when touring Europe), and how they would collect flowers and press them. All at once it seemed they had a dozen fascinating and vital projects.

"We'll be so happy!" declared Jacintha.

"The time will simply fly!"

"Now—" Jacintha got to her feet. "Thank you, and it's my turn to brush your hair."

"I'll run next door for my brush. I won't be a moment. . . ."

She hurried with quick little steps to the door, kissing the tips of her fingers to Jacintha as she went out. At the same instant Jacintha heard an unexpected sound behind her and felt a rush of air. She whirled swiftly, her flesh crawling with horror. Her stomach plunged as if a molten ball had dropped through it.

A door had opened in the floor at her feet, and there was Grant grinning up at her.

He grabbed her ankle. "Quick! Before she comes back!"

"Let go of me!" cried Jacintha. Frantically, she began trying to break away, struggling furiously. "I'm going to scream!"

"I'll break your goddamned neck if you do."

Grant jerked her leg so violently and viciously that she was almost thrown to the floor.

As she tried to regain her footing, he yanked her down the steep stairway beyond the trapdoor. On the small landing he gave her a shove that knocked her against the wall. Then he reached up, and the door crashed down above their heads.

Jacintha cringed against the wall, watching him and shuddering. He had left a lantern at the foot of the stairs, and she saw another narrow wooden staircase not very different from the one that had led into the cellar at home.

Suddenly, from above, Cherry's voice cried piteously. "Jacintha! Jacintha! Come back! *Jacintha!*" Her voice rose in a a mournful wail and then dissolved into sobs.

Jacintha opened her mouth to scream. Grant clapped his hand across her face and held it there, fastening the fingers of his other hand on her shoulder and giving her a hard push in the small of her back with his knee.

"Down the stairs!"

She turned and, at the sight of his angry, distorted face, picked up her skirts and went scurrying down as fast as she could. Even so, he gave her another shove that sent her sprawling the last half-dozen steps. She heard Cherry call to her once more, and then Grant seized her wrist, picked up the lantern, and pulled her along a narrow, winding stone passageway, far beneath the ground's surface. The air was cold and wet.

He went at such speed that she could only stumble headlong behind him. Then, when she had begun to feel that her lungs were parched and shriveled and that she could follow him no farther, he stopped suddenly, flung open a great arched door, and shoved her into a brilliantly lighted room.

Jacintha stood there, panting and blinking, massaging her aching arms. Her gown was disheveled, her hair fell carelessly about her face and over her breasts; she looked like a Victorian wood sprite, chased by a satyr.

Meanwhile, Grant was halfway across the room with his same furious stride.

"Oh, please!" cried Jacintha, picking up her skirts and rushing at him. "Don't leave me alone!"

He stopped, turning slowly to look her up and down. Under his glare of contempt Jacintha grew rigid.

He turned on his heel, closing the door and locking her in.

With a pounding heart, she began looking curiously about.

Like everything else she had seen today, the square room was of enormous size; otherwise, it bore no resemblance to any other part of the lodge. The colors were brilliant—red, yellow, green, blue, orange—but not garish, for they were worked in tile set in complex geometric mosaics covering the floor and walls.

The ceiling was thirty or forty feet high, surrounded

by a tiled walk. Small recesses opened onto it, each lavishly furnished with an arched entrance of carved and gilded pillars. Rich Oriental carpets were strewn about the ground floor. In the center of the room was a vast circular red velvet ottoman; above it, suspended by red silk cords, hung an enormous chandelier shimmering with thousands of colored stones, twirling and spinning and changing like a kaleidoscope. Fantastic carved and jeweled weapons hung upon the walls.

Jacintha shook her head in wonderment as she stared up and down and all around. The room seemed to ebb and flow, and the patterns and lights made her dizzy and disoriented.

She heard a burst of masculine laughter, jumped as if she had been hit with a rock, and, after turning excitedly this way and that, saw him standing twenty feet away. He had apparently just risen from a chair near the fireplace.

"Oh!" she cried. "You scared me again! Why do you always do that?"

He bowed slightly. "I apologize." Then, mockingly: "You weren't expecting to find me here?"

Disconcerted, Jacintha looked away, saw that her dressing gown had fallen so that one shoulder was bare, and she jerked it up again.

He had removed his dinner coat and tie and wore the black, satin-bound trousers and white shirt opened down the front. His hands were in his pockets, his head slightly lowered, and only the edges of his straight white teeth showed as he smiled at her.

"Why do you like to frighten people?" demanded Jacintha. "Why do you always appear by surprise?"

"Why do you regard surprises as necessarily unpleasant?"

"Why—I don't. I love surprises, nice ones." She gestured nervously and frowned. "What makes you ask such an absurd question?"

"If the question were absurd, you wouldn't be disturbed by it. You know what it is, Jacintha, as well as I. The human heart is always ready to fear misfortune—it is heavy with the weight of its own guilt."

"If we are guilty, it's you who makes us so!"

Again he smiled, and shrugged. She lowered her eyes and took up the blue satin ribbon tied around her waist in a bow, with streamers that hung to the floor. She began rolling it into a ball, pretending to concentrate as she did so.

"You had no dinner?" he asked.

She shook her head.

"Would you like something now? Old habits survive here . . . for a while."

She shook her head. She could not look at him. She was thinking of the sound of Cherry's voice, and it seemed she could hear it as clearly as if her mother were crying to her this moment: "Jacintha! Jacintha! Come back! *Jacintha!*"

The memory of that pitiful, pleading voice that had been like a piercing instrument down the flesh of her back, seemed to scrape along her bones.

I must get away from here somehow—I must get away at once and go back and tell her that I am not her rival and never want to be. I must get back to her now, this moment, so that she will know there was not possibly time.

There she stopped, and closed her eyes hard:

I must get back before I look at him again.

It's part of his depravity to look like that—brilliant and compelling. Even if he weren't who he is, he is too fantastically beautiful to be trusted.

I won't be fooled by it. I won't be taken in. No matter what happens, I won't look at him.

But even then the desire to have one more glimpse was growing stronger. Only one quick glimpse, to convince herself that she had exaggerated his beauty and his danger.

He was a handsome man, it was true. But no man was irresistible unless you wanted him to be—unless you gave him the gift of irresistibility. Brian had possessed great power over her, yet she had sensed then and knew clearly now that it was her own need that had endowed him with mystery and urgency.

If that was true, then this man could be no different.

I've let my imagination run away with me again.

While she stood, her eyes closed, frowning, he watched her silently. Then he picked up a pipe, filled and lighted it, and drew a slow, deep breath.

Jacintha opened her eyes and looked at him. He exhaled a cloud of smoke, allowing it to curl slowly from his nostrils, and it seemed to her that he stood in a boiling mist. Despite the room's tremendous size, he somehow created the impression of being bigger than his surroundings, of seeming to extend the boundaries of his personality until the room contained him and nothing else. The illusion was eerie and supernatural.

She blinked her eyes a few times; when she opened them and gave him a long, intense stare she found, to her relief, that he was the same size he had always been—it was a clue to her state of mind and one more warning.

"That fellow Grant!" she cried. "I think you should get rid of him." Her eyes looked bright and scared, but she faced him proudly. "He abused me coming here. He's cruel and loathsome and as ugly as a dead monkey."

He laughed, and his black eyes glittered with malicious amusement. "His orders are to get you here without any noticeable damage to your beauty. If he gives you a few cuffs along the way, he serves me well and I have no wish to interfere with his little pleasures."

"You don't *care* if he hurts me?"

"Did he hurt you?" he inquired in a reasonable tone. "He didn't leave you less beautiful to look at."

"Well!" That was the most outrageous thing she had ever heard.

Slowly Jacintha drew herself to her full height, raising her breasts, lifting her head, and staring steadily at him with hauteur and disdain. "Do you know that every time I encounter you, you become more obnoxious to me?" It was her most awesome, forbidding manner yet somehow, even to her, she sounded like a little girl wearing her mother's shoes and talking to herself in the mirror.

His hearty burst of laughter did not surprise her very

much, though it did embarrass her into looking at him
with all her assumed composure gone. He laid down the
pipe and started slowly toward her.

She watched him warily. With each step he took, she
found it more difficult to breathe. Terror began to run
through her body, like wind chasing a prairie fire. Slowly,
steadily, implacably, he was advancing on her. The sound
of his footsteps on the bare tiles seemed to echo thunder-
ously in the vast, silent room.

He loomed larger and larger, and she felt sure that he
would envelop and crush her. She stood staring at him,
shaking; her fear became a heedless stampede. She gasped
and her hands reached out. She tried to cry aloud but only
moaned, as in a nightmare.

His size and presence faded abruptly; he blurred and
vanished. At the same time, a distant ringing in her ears
began; cold sweat broke out on her forehead and over her
face and neck. Her eyes closed and she swayed forward.

He took a few quick running steps and caught her in
his arms, then tenderly held her against him, supporting
her head with one hand. When, after a time, she raised
her head, he instantly released her.

*Oh, why does he make everything so difficult? What-
ever is going to happen, should happen now. What is he
waiting for?*

She looked up at him once more.

He was shaking his head, slightly smiling, but the
look of malice had gone. "You Victorians. Here . . . sit
down. Try to compose yourself."

Jacintha silently obeyed. She sat at the far end of the

low, deep ottoman, backing up against the corner. She sat very straight with her delicate hands resting relaxed with palms upward in her lap, her ankles lightly crossed. She looked as if she expected to be catechized. Still, she felt much easier. His gentleness was reassuring.

Although she felt resentful that he had dragged her here in this unceremonious fashion, she found herself guiltily pleased to be with him and full of eager anticipation for what the next moment would produce.

She cast him a worried sidelong glance. He gave her a quick smile and, after a moment's surprise, she spontaneously responded with a childlike smile and a little laugh.

"Tell me," he said, after a moment. "Have you enjoyed your reunion with your mother?"

Jacintha's face grew suddenly red. She had been on the point of flirting with him. In fact, she had been flirting with him. That little laugh was one of her most valuable assets—she had never met a man who was not charmed by it. This was his sly way of reminding her.

"Of course." She arched her brows and looked at him disdainfully. "It's been a wonderful thing to find each other again. We thought at first that it was a happy coincidence, but then of course realized it was a trick of yours." Her eyes narrowed accusingly. "You know that she is madly in love with you, don't you?"

"I know that she says she loves me. I'm not sure what she means by it."

"I know what she means by it. If you don't know what love is, I pity you."

"As it happens, I've never been altogether convinced that any of you know what you mean by it."

"I'll tell you then: love is the emotion that completes life."

He was watching her steadily, and she felt the anxiety return. In mobilizing all her forces, the frantic mood swings of alternately drawing together and falling apart had left her in helpless consternation.

"You want to make me fall in love with you, too, don't you?" she demanded after a long pause. "Then you intend to amuse yourself by seeing how much trouble we will have over you."

He raised his eyebrows in mocking admiration but did not reply.

"We saw through your trick. I suppose that surprises you. Most likely you think you're much too crafty for anyone else to understand."

Her speech gave her a glow of pride and pleasure. She felt that her mind was brilliant, her emotions large and noble, her beauty sparkling and fresh, and that, all in all, he must be more chagrined than he had ever been in his long and infamous career with women.

Still he said nothing for a moment or so and then, slowly, he said, "After all, I have to occupy my time, too."

Jacintha, to her own surprise, gave a sudden, gleeful little laugh and clapped her hands together. "You see!" she cried joyously. "I knew it! I saw through you."

"So you did," he agreed.

But now she felt deprived of her triumph. It was as if she had been holding a red balloon and suddenly it was gone. How had he done that?

"Shall I go now?" she asked him, and stood up.

"Do you want to?"

"Of course I want to! You've just admitted . . . everything."

"Go on, then."

"The door is locked. Grant locked it when we came in."

She had expected him to tell her to sit down and behave herself and felt as if she had been pulling on a rope with all her strength, only to have him suddenly let go and send her staggering back, trying to catch her balance.

"It's open. Run along."

He got to his feet and stood with his hands in his pockets again, watching her and waiting. The initiative was hers.

She must somehow manage to leave this room with dignity and pride and the firm conviction that, no matter what her present company and surroundings, she was a Victorian lady, wellborn and well-bred.

She stood for a moment as if at a court function, regarding him with imperious disdain, then turned slowly, her gown swirling over the floor in a semicircle, and, with her hair streaming, her ruffled skirt billowing, she started with stately steps to cross the room.

Her progress to the door was an increasing humiliation. She was agonizingly aware of him watching her with his black eyes blazing with mockery. She felt as though the muscles along her backbone were spasmodically jumping, like keys on a player piano.

When she had gone about ten yards she stopped, clasped her fingers hard together, drew in a deep breath—and turned to confront him. He was standing in exactly the same place, the same position, looking at her with the same expression.

"Have you never had respect," she began, dismayed to hear the high, quavering pitch of her voice, "for any woman?"

He smiled slightly, but almost instantly, seeing how hurt she was, his face sobered and he shook his head.

"Respect," he said, in a pleasant, friendly tone, "is a state of mind forced on children by their parents. Of what use is it to an adult? Respect implies subservience to my mind. Grant, for example. He respects me greatly. He's afraid I'd kick his balls off . . . if he still had them."

Jacintha was curiously pleased to hear of Grant's deprivation. It was the least he deserved. Then, remembering something she had heard or read: "Even a castrated man can still have a woman."

"Not with my method, he can't. As I told you, having been put in charge here by, we suppose, superior powers, I have arranged things to my liking."

Jacintha listened carefully. There was something new in his voice—something . . . what could it be?

It was like a caress. The very tones seemed to stroke her arms and back and breasts, despite the distance between them—tenderly, steadily, voluptuously—making her warm and luxurious. Was he putting off immortality?

Whatever he said to her, outrageous as it would have seemed in her other world, even upon her first arrival in this one, had begun instead to sound logical, often amusing. She was beginning to enter into a conspiracy with him: the two of them, against her earlier life, her earlier convictions. And prejudices?

He came toward her with a quickness that was almost uncanny. He moves like an animal, she thought, as if that were one more thing to keep in mind against him. A gentleman should be graceful—but not as graceful, certainly, as a panther.

Jacintha whirled, turning her back on him, and covered her face with her hands. She was suddenly so frightened that she began to tremble, and the trembling increased until she stood shivering helplessly, her hands over her face.

"Tell me," he said finally. "What are you afraid of?"

She felt his hand touch her left forearm, very gently, and the fingers closed with tenderness and care.

Gradually the trembling stopped, and she raised her head and waited, alert as a trapped fawn in a field, scenting imminent danger. Desire grabbed at her heart like a closing fist. She stood perfectly still now, waiting for what he would do. His size, boundless and unconquerable, seemed to increase as she shrank, becoming smaller and progressively more helpless.

Very slowly, with exaggerated tenderness, he turned her face to his and, at last, the mockery was gone from his eyes. He was looking down at her and his expression was sober, though not unduly serious. He seemed to wish, to will, that she be afraid of him no longer.

His resplendent male beauty seemed no longer a threat, but a generous benefaction, meant for her pleasure and enjoyment.

The edges of her mouth trembled upward in a tentative smile, and the smile was reflected on his face.

She continued looking at him questioningly, afraid to trust him for fear the mockery would return. But, as it did not, her smile grew wider until her lips parted over her white teeth, her eyes sparkled with merriment, and all at once she flung back her head and laughed. In another moment he was laughing with her, and they were transported by mirth, rejoicing and exultant. Finally there seemed some profound understanding between them.

Even as she laughed, she was vaguely aware that this rapturous delight and exhilaration had resulted from nothing more remarkable than his taking her by the arm and turning her face to him. His domination, accomplished by tenderness rather than by force, was so complete that she now wished only to please him and to continue this marvelous sense of buoyant felicity which his smile, frank and devoid of mockery, had produced.

She felt that finally he approved of her, that he found her most beautiful when she looked happy and content, without fear in her eyes or distrust in her expression.

"There," he said at last. "How lovely you look now."

"I do?" she whispered. "Oh—thank you."

She knew that she had passed by imperceptible degrees into a state of devoted mesmerism. She had succumbed to him as completely as she had ever wished or believed she had surrendered to Brian. He had cast some magical enchantment over her with the sound of his voice and his heroic masculinity.

For surely, there must have been something else— some necromancy at play to magnetize a woman of her rather cool or, at least, composed temperament, a woman who had found only one genuine passion during her life, but a few months before her death.

Well, then, she was a victim of sorcery. There was no use imagining or hoping any longer that she could contest with him.

"Are you sure," he asked her, "that you have ever been in love before?"

"Before?" she repeated. "Then you think that I am in love with you now?"

"Aren't you?"

His hand left her shoulder and moved slowly around to her back, pressing against her flesh; his fingers fastened in her hair and drew her head backward, pulling with a steady strength. The pain became pleasurable so that she neither winced nor cried out, but only continued to stand with her head back, looking into his face with an expression of reverence and gratitude, humble almost to abjectness.

She would have dropped to her knees at that moment and prayed to him, if he had not been holding her. She

was ashamed to realize that she actually wished to kneel at
his feet.

"I never felt before," she murmured, "as I do toward
you. It's . . . uncanny. I seem to have lost my pride; and I
was always very proud. I was even proud of being proud."

"Then you were never in love. One thing a woman
cannot keep if she loves a man, is her pride. Pride is a
ridiculous encumbrance for a woman if she ever hopes to
feel anything more than pleasant titillation. Pride is an
emotion suitable to a man's sense of conquest—so what
would a woman be doing with it?"

"I don't know," whispered Jacintha. "I can't imagine now. I think, though, that I was trying to rid myself of
it when I fell in love with Brian. My husband was never
able to take it from me. I always felt superior to him."

He released her abruptly. She had been depending on
him so completely for support that she staggered slightly;
he caught her by one arm to steady her for a moment, then
let her go. He turned, walked several steps from her, and
slowly faced her again. She stood gazing wistfully after
him, her brown eyes puzzled and hurt. Her arms fell
gracefully at her sides, the skirt of her ruffled gown swept
in front of her, like swirling water.

"I think that you must have been quite eager to get
here. What was it you heard about me that made you so
anxious to meet me?"

Jacintha was astonished. A moment ago he had been
making love to her. Now, suddenly, he had abandoned
her and gone back to casual conversation. Having con-

95

quered her so easily, perhaps he had lost interest and was not even going to pursue his conquest to its logical termination.

Jacintha longed to run to him, beg him to look at her as he had before, to touch her and kiss her. But she was afraid. As soon as he moved away, something of her old pride seemed to return, warning her not to make a fool of herself, or he would lose any regard he might have for her.

Play his game. Smile and flirt and talk to him as he seems to want. Please him—and, if you please him enough—he will give you what you want.

That's the terrible thing about being a woman. It's the waiting. You can never take what you want, as a man can, but you must wait for it to be given to you. All your life is spent in coaxing, wheedling, fawning, pandering, enticing, stimulating, flirting—all the petty roundabout ways a woman must travel to reach her goal.

And, even here, it is the same.

She smiled at him and made a pretty little gesture with one hand, tossing back the hair from her face, shaking her head so that its long, springy mass swung and bobbed behind her. She answered his question in a soft, low voice—the tone Brian had told her was as lulling and distracting as whatever song it may have been the sirens used to sing.

"I heard what everyone does about you, I suppose. What makes you think I was eager to meet you?" She spoke with pert provocativeness, offering herself by her manner, proclaiming her independence by her words.

"You've fallen in love with me so quickly. I have to conclude you were in love with me before we met." He shrugged. "There must have been something you heard. You heard I was handsome?"

"I heard you were ugly."

He laughed. "You heard I was fascinating to women?"

"I heard you were repulsive." She laughed triumphantly in return.

"You heard I could give a woman greater pleasure than any other man?"

"I heard there was nothing more terrible than to be . . . than to be . . . with you."

He was still laughing. "So that's the way you were brought up! No wonder men were such a disappointment to you. Well, I never thought sex should be available to everyone."

"What?"

"Of course not. I have a sense of the fitness of things, a sense of aesthetics, if you will, and it disgusts me to see the way such things are managed on earth, where everyone has both equipment and inclination. To picture the ordinary couple at their lovemaking is enough to turn your stomach, isn't it?"

"I've never thought about it," she lied.

"Well, I have. And I don't like what I see. And so I've arranged things differently here."

"You've arranged . . . How, for heaven's sake?"

"I don't let any unattractive women in the main

lodge, to begin with, because I can't stand the sight of them. And the unattractive men—I have them castrated. They make very good lackeys, if somewhat surly ones, like Grant.''

Jacintha reflected and was surprised to hear herself say, "It's not a bad idea, you know.'' She smiled.

He laughed softly, while his eyes were searching her eyes, over her lips, across her smooth skin. "You are not nearly so moral as that world you lived in forced you to pretend. I think you may have liked the idea of adultery more than you liked Brian.''

"I loved Brian!''

"I'm sure you did, so far as you knew. But you wanted to be superior to the time you lived in. It's the same with every one of you. You are all rebels. Petty ones, for the most part, when I consider my own rebellion.'' He shrugged. "Still, I suppose it's better than no rebellion at all.'' Now he was smiling at her with a look of brooding tenderness. "You know, you have a wonderful mouth. And that's very important to an earthy bastard like me.''

Where was the immortality now? Vanished for the time being? Its loss made him no less imposing.

Jacintha caught her breath and stood perfectly still, gazing up at him with a rapt, helpless stare, her fingers laced together for support. She seemed to be reeling about the room in swift spirals. Finally, when she stopped spinning, she gave a gentle sigh and lowered her lashes demurely.

"Thank you.'' She glanced up quickly to see his amused smile.

"My husband thought I had a cold nature," she confided. "Of course, he thought I *should* have," she amended.

"You must have had a fine life with him. There's no such thing as a woman who is cold by nature. By accident, perhaps—but never by nature. That's a contradiction in terms."

"Oh, do you think so?" whispered Jacintha.

She was beginning to feel a reckless, rushing excitement. Her breath was coming quicker; her lips were parted in eager anticipation; her hands were held before her breasts, palms together. Surely there was something miraculous in the way he was standing and talking to her, with that easy, friendly smile and manner, not mocking her, not speaking as if she were a pretty child: telling her of the lies that had ruled her life. It must be wrong to listen—yet it was intoxicating. He might have been lying himself, but it didn't matter; she would have believed anything he told her.

"However," he continued, "you won't find any of your men admitting that, since it is the myth of female reticence and comparative coldness that bolsters their own crippled self-esteem. A man who is sure of himself—and there can't be many in your kind of world—knows that any woman can be brought to heel as eagerly as his hunting spaniel. The others, who trust themselves less, must believe in a woman's inferior ardor."

She listened, absorbing the words, swept by a rapturous enthusiasm for this moment when they seemed so safely and honestly close together. It was as if she had been granted something for which she had longed her whole life, without knowing it: she had been welcomed into a man's friendly confidence and treated by him as if she merited his respect. For the first time she realized that the men who had loved her always kept the barrier of her femininity between them. He, on the other hand, had brought them closer together by his appreciation of it.

She had forgotten Cherry.

She no longer believed that he was evil or cruel.

She had become perfectly submissive, ruled by an unashamed and elemental adoration.

His beauty appeared to her more glorious than ever before, his power prodigious: swift, vibrant, supreme. Jacintha's face wore an exquisite look of aspiration and homage.

Before her eyes his expression altered, and for the first time she saw pure, exultant lust in a man's eyes. At the sudden appearance of this primal ruthlessness, she became aware that every man she had ever known, and the two men who had loved her, had been liars. At that moment everything that had composed her pride, her feminine expectancy of respect and tenderness, collapsed. There was nothing left of it, and no certain hope of repair.

Several moments passed, very slowly, it seemed, as she stood transfixed, lost in her new awareness of the world. The quality of this man's desire was primordial and ferocious, a thronging lust which would surge over her like a herd of wild horses, pounding her into annihilation.

Then she heard a distantly echoing roar, followed by

sullen rumbling. Glancing toward a line of windows near the ceiling, she saw spasmodic bursts of lightning. A storm was beginning.

Jacintha reacted to this natural tumult with an increased surge of painful anxiety, for the lightning seemed to heighten her excitement. She wanted to turn and run from him. She had a vision of herself beginning to run, of him starting in pursuit, of her dissolving through the wall as she reached it, leaving him baffled and helpless.

She sensed, in his desire, the threat of her own final destruction. He would accomplish what her death had not. Her death had been sudden and final, but she had somehow remained aloof from it. Whereas, if this man took her body, she would be forced to participate, to be continuously aware; she would have to experience whatever sensations he chose to inflict on her. She would be his passive victim, with the great danger that he might arouse her so violently that she would demolish herself, responding to her own passion.

Very slowly, her arms reached out, as if she were begging for charity. Her head was tilted slightly back so that the fine, long line of her throat showed in clear relief, while the twirling chandelier cast multicolored lights across her face and shoulders.

"Please . . ." she whispered. "Let me go . . . let me . . ."

He took a quick step and was close beside her, looking down into her face, his own expression serious and brooding but mingled with a strange tenderness.

"Why are you afraid?" he asked her. "Why are you less courageous now than when you were alive?"

He smiled and was so close that she felt herself engulfed by the smell of his body, the sheen across his white teeth, and the texture of his skin.

"Because—I'm in love with you." She was surprised to hear the words and wondered vaguely where they had come from and how it had happened they were spoken in her voice.

"Don't be."

"Don't be in love. . . ?"

"Love is jealous, and jealousy closes the world. Love is possessive, intolerant."

Having given her that advice, he proceeded to make it impossible for her to heed it.

His face was moving downward, still with that faint smile. His mouth touched hers, softly and lightly, and the next moment seemed ready to devour her. Stunned by this remorseless energy, Jacintha tried to step backward and found herself locked against his body.

She experienced a moment of panic. Her control was gone. She had a sense of profound despair—and the premonition that in another moment she would disintegrate.

Far above, through the black windows, shone a blinding flash and there was presently a sound of distant booming. The storm was steadily approaching, like a giant striding over the mountains.

While one arm held her fast against him, his free

hand moved slowly down her back, leaving in its wake a spreading glow, as her body grew warm with a craving to match his. Her arms strained to hold him closer, her head turned restlessly from side to side. She made unconscious sounds of moaning and felt herself disappear into this warm, rough embrace, his lips feeding on hers as if at a delicious spring.

The Victorian lady had vanished, momentarily replaced by a tormented woman, and even that pretense had gone, leaving only a quickened anonymous female.

His hands unfastened her garments easily and they fell into a heap. He released her to fling his shirt aside and then his trousers, and stood naked at last, blazing with supernatural beauty and power.

Marveling, she gazed at that proud masculine display, the male blossom of flesh and blood, which had never failed to arouse her awe and wonder.

She knelt on the ottoman before him and took it into her hands, the magical object, almost a separate being, and put her lips to the hard, glistening tip. Then, bowing her head, forgetful of them both in her helpless idolatry, she ran her hands slowly over his legs, long and splendidly formed, not heavy of thigh or calf but as beautiful as everything else about him.

The storm grew suddenly louder and more violent. Streaks of glaring light illuminated the windows and lashed through the room. Thunder roared, as if to blow this place open. The wind howled in piercing tones; rain came pouring over the windows.

Now his face wore a wild and brilliant smile that seemed part of the storm itself. Suddenly he laughed:

"Lust is a wonderful thing, isn't it?"

His arms reached out and drew her to him. He swept the hair off her neck and put his mouth there.

Yes, it is a wonderful thing. I never knew what it was. I never dared to know—and I never met anyone who could teach me.

He seized her wrist in a light, strong grip, twisted her deftly about, and she was lying on the ottoman. For a moment she looked up and saw him above her, his face in darkness, and felt a paralyzing terror, a conviction that he would destroy her, tear her body, burst her asunder.

He knelt across her and gently forced her backward. "Take all the pleasure you can," he told her, his voice low and serious, "from every moment," and as he entered her a sensation of warmth and delight flowed to all the parts of her body, until even her throat turned hot and her wrists seemed to burn. She experienced a sharp, clear joy, a feeling of intense aliveness and, with it, the sorrowful but unmourned recognition that she would never again be able to claim herself.

There was a vague resentment, a passing desire to protect her freedom, and then she felt herself melting, ready to experience whatever lay ahead.

Slowly he moved inside her, slowly and thoughtfully. Her eyes were closed. The side of his head pressed hers and his face was hidden in her hair. Their breathing came, simultaneously, in tight gasps. Their bodies moved with the same rhythm. All sense of time disappeared in a welter of sensation, and she was hopelessly aware of a newfound desire that he could never satisfy. She envisioned herself enduring this same, steadily increasing torment forever.

With increasing keenness, feeling that she had been mounted by a ruthless rider who drove her steadily toward an exquisite climax, she had lost all awareness of Jacintha Frost.

She had some dim sense of the storm building to a greater and greater frenzy. Boisterously it battered the lodge, swept in violent gusts—rending, rioting, smashing. Nothing could survive its rage. The building must crack apart, the land would be broken and devastated. Jacintha became unable to distinguish between the storm as it brawled around them and the storm surging through her body.

She had been crying, perhaps for some time, and all at once she heard sobs, distracted cries of pleasure and hopelessness, the pleasure for its own sake, the hopelessness for the knowledge that it must end.

She caught a glimpse of his face, dark and shining, with a strange, triumphant smile; yet it was a smile of anguish, and in a moment even that had vanished to leave her only the brief sight he had warned her of—the haggard and distraught face of mortal man enduring the last struggles of passion. He seemed to be consciously aware of her slightest desire and responded at once, driving them both to heightened pleasure and agony.

Their avidity grew keener, with a fine edge of ruthlessness to it, not quite cruelty, but a sensual abandonment she had begun to believe would never end. They would remain locked together, throbbing, moving at this remorseless pace, as if they had been joined into one being.

He was thrusting into her with increasingly swift strokes, and as she clasped him harder with her arms and legs, she felt the beginning pulse, the beat of him inside her, and the pouring, surging charge which left her shuddering and weakened.

Her body seemed to dissolve into his, as very slowly, he became quieter and lay full upon her, seemingly unconscious. She trembled uncertainly between awareness and annihilation, and then swam surely into a welcoming oblivion.

Jacintha slowly, lazily regained consciousness. Her mind came back to the surface, surprised to find that she had survived. Her fear was gone; there was only a deep gratitude. They seemed to have gone on a long, venturesome voyage, shared its dangers and marvels, and returned with a common experience that would bind them forever.

She opened her eyes and looked about the room. There he stood, fully dressed in evening clothes, looking into a mirror as he knotted his tie. He glanced at her and smiled, a confiding smile, seeming to confirm her own hopes.

"I feel," she murmured, "as if I had been dead and come to life again." She laughed, and all at once sat up. "I was afraid—terrified—at first. I have never been so afraid. . . ."

He answered her gently. "If a woman doesn't feel some fear, she won't feel great pleasure, either." He came to stand beside her, and she looked up confidently. She would never lose him again. He touched her hair and said, "Yes, it's very strong—very deep." There was thoughtfulness in his voice—and sorrow. "And if it should continue, these early sensations will seem ephemeral. Each time there will be new pleasures, more intense, nearly intolerable—"

"It is nearly intolerable now."

He smiled. How easily he had taken her.

But now she felt his hand pass gently across her shoulder, his mouth briefly touched her wet face, and it was a moment before she realized that he had said, "Good night. Sleep well." By then, he was halfway across the great room.

She sprang up and started after him. "Don't leave me!" she cried despairingly.

He might have heard her, or he might not, but he had disappeared through one of the innumerable doors opening out of this vast chamber.

For a moment Jacintha stood motionless, and then, as if in response to some unspoken command, she sat on the ottoman, lay back, and was asleep again.

She had no idea how long she slept, for when she woke, sitting up and looking swiftly about, everything was the same, even the slowly turning kaleidoscope of lights over her head. And there was silence: not a sound of any kind. The storm had passed.

She got quickly to her feet, moving lightly and with fluent grace, finding herself refreshed, filled with a sparkling strength.

The sensation was miraculous, and within a moment she realized it was the gift he had left her, the residue of his imperial power which had entered her own blood and muscles.

She looked down at her naked body. She had always admired her beauty, but now it seemed he had transformed her, made her more lovable to her self.

She began to move quickly about the room, searching, looking behind pillars, between archways. The room was empty.

There was an unexpected sound. She turned sharply to see the door open and Grant come in. She cried out warningly, and with a hasty feminine movement sought to cover her body with her hands.

"Get out of here! Don't you dare stand there staring at me!"

He was indeed staring at her, but with no more interest than he had shown when she was dressed. "Put your clothes on! Hurry up!"

"I'll have you beaten! Things have changed since you saw me last."

At that he gave a mocking, contemptuous laugh which startled her like a shot. There was an unpleasant premonition in it. Now he was swaggering toward her and, since she could not frighten him away, Jacintha snatched her clothes and stood behind a tall-backed chair while she dressed.

He walked about aimlessly, scuffling his feet, kicking at carpets and furniture, a scowl on his face and his hands in his pockets, like the ill-natured middle-aged brat he appeared to be.

"I'm ready!"

He stopped his ramble, glanced at her as she stepped from behind the chair, then shuffled toward the great door through which they had entered—how long ago?

She walked slowly toward him. "I'll do as you say now," she informed him imperiously. "But later— he will hear about you."

Grant shrugged. He opened the door and gave a jerk of his head to indicate that she should precede him. She swept disdainfully by and he picked up a lantern which threw ragged shadows about the black, narrow passage. They came to the foot of the stairs, and there she stopped, white and cold: *Cherry.*

Was Cherry at the top of those stairs, waiting?

She had forgotten her so completely that it was now a greater shock than it had been to meet her again after their separation of twenty years.

Jacintha recalled with agonizing vividness Cherry's lucid little face, gazing up at him as they stood together in the lobby. She could see the troubled look come into her eyes. She could hear her talking, merrily chattering, trying not to betray her desperation.

And then, Grant had summoned her and she had gone—against her will, firmly intending to remain faithful to the promise she had made Cherry and herself.

She hesitated, stunned to have found herself capable

of such treachery. Then, as she felt a hard shove at her back, she stumbled forward, throwing out her hands against the steps above.

She turned, and there was his grotesque face, just beneath her, waiting with his air of violent impatience.

"I *can't* go up there!" she told him tensely. "Don't make me go back up there, I beg of you. I'll give you all my jewelry—I'll—"

"Quick! I've wasted time enough on you. I've got other business."

She stood where she was, staring down at him with cold determination. But after a moment, he gave a grunting laugh and, with a sudden motion, raised his arm, threatening to strike her. She gave an involuntary shriek and turned, started up, and the door was flung wide, as if blown open by a gale. She ran to the top as fast as she could and arrived breathless in her own room. She had one last glimpse of Grant's face, grinning as he slammed the door. She peered closely, but its outline had been lost in the riotous flower garden that decorated the carpet.

Then, swiftly, she turned.

The room was empty.

That was both such relief and shock that she began to tremble and perspire and, after a moment, had to sit down, weak and almost sick. She sat there and slowly shook her head, back and forth, back and forth. Tears dropped gently upon her hands as they lay folded in her lap.

In their excitement last night, they had forgotten to

draw the draperies, and now the room was growing light. Slowly she rose and went to look out the eastern windows. There was a pink streak along the edges of the dark, distant mountains, and in the vague milky light she could see steam rising, faintly blue and red and green. She leaned her forehead against the glass to feel its coolness, then pressed her cheek and finally her lips against it as she stood there, gazing wistfully out. She could hear the cawing of hoarse-throated birds, keeping up a steady complaint, and before her floated a magpie, his feathers so floppy she smiled at him with tender amusement.

She stood for several minutes gazing out, forlorn and perplexed. The time she and Cherry had spent together yesterday now seemed far longer than an afternoon and evening; it had contained the real beginning, the culmination, and the end of their relationship as mother and daughter.

She had forfeited, through her selfishness and treachery, any claim she had ever had to Cherry's love. And now she must confront eternity alone, as she deserved—comfortless, desolate.

Her muted feelings were of mournful disillusionment and regret.

When I've slept I will go to her and apologize, even though I know she won't accept it and shouldn't accept it. Still, it's my duty to humble myself. Or perhaps something will happen which will make it unnecessary for me to do anything at all.

Jacintha wandered from window to window, drawing

the heavy crimson draperies until at last the room was dark. She undressed, got into bed naked, and stretched out on her back, her hands flung above her head, palms open and fingers curled like a child's, eyes closed.

I'll think about him.

Now that it's done, I can't undo it by refusing to think about him. I've done the worst thing I can—and, in a way, that leaves me free. . . .

These were strange thoughts, quite unlike any she had had while scheming to spend a stolen hour or two with Brian. Then, she had brooded over her sin, haunted by her thoughts, wondering where the evil streak in her nature had come from.

Now, even her remorse had in it some pride. She found that she could recall him with startling clarity. There was not a detail of his looks, a tone of his voice, a word he had said, a gesture, any of the violent, exuberant emotions he had made her feel that she would ever forget. He was vividly present.

As she was falling asleep, she recalled with tenderness and gratitude everything that had happened between them—from the moment she had turned and found him standing smiling down at her, almost naked against the brilliant sun striking off Roaring Mountain.

She remembered the crispness between her fingers of the black curly hairs covering his chest. She smelled his breath and tasted his mouth. She felt the hard muscles of his back, spasmodically working as he pumped his energy into her. She cherished every sensation with such intensity that again and again she was swept by waves of passion. Her desire for him had returned in full demanding force, treacherously threatening to drive her into frantic despair. At that moment she experienced a horrified revulsion.

She felt sickened with love and yearning and dismay: *I am bewitched or insane.* Her eyes searched desperately through the dark room.

Surely it is unhealthy for a woman to feel this kind of desire. It's immodest and unladylike. It leaves me helpless and incomplete, a faceless female, waiting and hoping. He will return—when it pleases him to. I am at the mercy of his whims.

I must get over this ridiculous idolatry. Surely, the next time I see him he will repel me. No man can arouse such violent, atavistic feelings without finally growing repulsive.

Her face twisted.

I think perhaps he is ugly, after all— Yes, I'm sure that he is. . . .

She now converted her emotions into depraved, unnatural feelings. He had employed some trick to take away her femininity and pride and natural dignity.

And he had succeeded, until this moment when some lingering sense of decency was making her consider what had happened.

How stupid he must think I am.

How he must laugh at me and despise me.

She brushed her hand through the darkness, as though to banish his malignant image. He had enchanted her; nevertheless, she had both the strength and the courage to break the enchantment and set herself free. Finally she slept.

Jacintha awoke to find Cherry's face above her. She looked up, only mildly surprised, and then, slowly and softly, she smiled. For the moment, she forgot everything but the image of her beloved mother's face.

Cherry was leaning across her, fully dressed for an outing of some kind. She held a small, closed parasol in one hand. Her gown, which fit with fashionable tightness, was of bright green-and-red plaid wool, buttoned down the front, with a black velvet collar; and there was a little black velvet bonnet perched on top of her head. She smelled, as she always had, of some fresh lilac fragrance, and Jacintha thought that she looked captivating.

"Aren't you ever going to get up?" Cherry gently chided.

Still smiling, Jacintha yawned and stretched and started to reply. Then her smile disappeared; her dark eyes widened and, involuntarily, she stuck one forefinger into her mouth, like a little girl expecting to be punished. Cherry continued to gaze down at her, calm and compassionate, and Jacintha, unable to endure the absence of blame in her eyes, turned suddenly upon her belly and hid her face in her arms, sobbing.

Almost instantly she felt the pressure of Cherry's bosom upon her back, and Cherry's arms around her. Her hands began to stroke and smooth the tangle of her black hair, and her voice was light and comforting.

"No, no, no," she murmured. "Don't cry, my darling—please don't cry. You mustn't cry."

Jacintha, sobbing now, looked up at Cherry across her naked shoulder. Her face was wet with tears, and her expression mingled pleading with horror.

"You hate me now!" she sobbed, crying so hard she could scarcely breathe. Cherry took a handkerchief from the little black velvet bag which hung at her wrist and began to blot Jacintha's face. "You do hate me! I *know* you hate me! And you should—you're right to—I deserve it! Oh," she wailed, "I hate myself."

Cherry, still blotting the tears that continued to pour down her daughter's cheeks, answered gently. "No, Jacintha. I don't blame you. How can I blame you?"

"How can you *not* blame me?"

She had an almost furious need for Cherry's blame and hatred, for some swift, shattering punishment. If only Cherry would recoil from her, speak to her with bitterness and contempt, abandon her to eternal loneliness and despair.

Sighing, Cherry gave her the handkerchief and stood up. "It's a beautiful day. You get dressed and we'll go for a stroll—or perhaps a picnic. They have delightful picnic spots here." As she talked she was drawing the cords so that the draperies swung back and brilliant light flooded the room. Jacintha had to cover her eyes until she became accustomed to it. Cherry brought her wrapper to her. "Come now, darling—do get up. It's such a glorious day. It always is here when there's been a great storm the night before."

Jacintha, sitting on the edge of the bed and slipping

into her wrapper, felt her face suddenly burn. Her face and neck turned red, and there was a nervous prickling in her armpits; it seemed that her ears were erect and waiting for what Cherry would say next. Though she did not know why, the storm seemed intimately connected with everything that had happened.

Jacintha stood, drawing the wrapper about her, and paused in the doorway, not quite looking toward Cherry. "How long did the storm—"she began, and then stopped, afraid that Cherry would know why she asked— "last?" she finished recklessly, for she had an obsessive need to know the answer.

There was a moment's silence. Jacintha, in alarm, glanced quickly at Cherry and found her smiling and gazing directly at her, with an expression quite different from any Jacintha had seen on her mother's face before. It was subtle and mysterious and tinged in some way with both cruelty and triumph. Jacintha's reaction was a quick, flashing spasm of fear, for this look now fastened on her was oddly sinister.

How strange and sad that Cherry should look at me like that. When only a moment ago she . . . she must have been reminding herself that she is my mother.

"The storm," Cherry replied, "lasted for three hours and a half."

Jacintha lowered her head and started through the doorway.

"I think you might be interested to know," continued Cherry, still in that same soft, but now, peculiarly malevolent tone, "that it always storms when he is making love."

"It does?"

She turned swiftly, went into the bathroom, and closed the door. There she stood for several moments, her muscles quivering and aching, as if some poison had been poured into them.

Three hours and a half! My God, how horrible! Oh, no, I won't think about it. I'll never think about it again. Does anyone but Cherry know I was with him last night? Oh, this is dreadful. It's a nightmare of everything I ever feared or despised.

She ran water into the tub and scrubbed herself vigorously and angrily. Then, she felt a little better.

She slipped back into her wrapper and returned to find Cherry sitting and smiling affectionately at herself in the little fan-shaped mirror, preening, tilting her head first to one side and then to the other. Though it was her own beauty Cherry was admiring, the expression was familiar, the same mixture of playful enjoyment and approval that Jacintha's own reflection assumed in the mirror. The satisfaction of being a beautiful woman was considerable. Jacintha always believed that everything of significance had occurred because of her beauty.

"You do look lovely today," she said shyly to Cherry, pausing a moment at the threshold.

How impossible it is—the way he has arranged things. After all, we are mother and daughter.

"Thank you, darling," said Cherry lightly, and

smiled at Jacintha who saw, to her measureless relief, that there was nothing left of that subtle, mysterious look that had made her so uneasy. "I've ordered a lunch made up for us. My maid is getting it now. We'll find some pretty forest or meadow for our picnic, and we can do some botanizing, too. This is the most wonderful place for it!"

Jacintha began to get dressed, as quickly as possible in spite of the layers of petticoats, the boned and laced corset, the dozens of hooks and pins that she wore under her gowns.

She marveled once more at how Cherry—after twenty years in this place and with an eternity ahead to contemplate—could be so optimistic, so happy in her manner, so enthusiastic and gay. She must try to match this lighthearted behavior, or she would infect them both with her own gloomy forebodings. She had been inclined, due no doubt to a vivid and active imagination, to spells of melancholy. In life, these dark moods were considered becoming and a fascinating aspect of her mysterious temperament. But here, where the cause of depression was so real and so terrible, she could not permit herself the luxury of such self-indulgence. She would harm Cherry as well as herself if she looked grave or seemed disconsolate.

And so, when Cherry spoke of botanizing, she took up the suggestion with a lively display of eagerness. "Oh, yes. I love flora! Father used to tell me how much you had enjoyed studying them, and I loved botany for your sake. Oh, I pursued it very seriously, I assure you."

They both laughed, and Cherry came over to lace her

corset and carefully arrange the curling tendrils along the nape of her neck. When she had finished, Jacintha turned with sudden impulsiveness—feeling the same overwhelming love she had the day before—and hugged Cherry close for a moment.

"Thank you. Thank you for not hating me."

"Shh," whispered Cherry. "We won't speak of it anymore. We *must* not speak of it anymore," she added, with gentle emphasis.

Jacintha stood looking down, a wistful smile playing at the corners of her mouth. "How splendid you are. If only I had you during the years I was growing up . . ."

Cherry made a pretext of gay laughter. "But, if you had . . . we would not be together here, would we?"

"No, we wouldn't."

"Or as we are," added Cherry, "both the same age."

Jacintha blushed at that delicate reminder of recent betrayal. After a moment, she quelled her feelings of self-consciousness and looked directly at Cherry with the most intense and dedicated expression.

"I promise you, it will never happen again."

Cherry shook her head and turned away. "Don't make promises. They don't mean anything here. They never mean anything when our strongest feelings threaten them. You don't know him yet."

"I know as much about him as I ever shall."

"Jacintha, please," said Cherry softly. "Let's talk about other things. There is only one subject dangerous to us. Why can't we avoid it?"

Jacintha nodded in silent obedience and finished dressing. Once more they began to talk lightly and frivolously and kept their conversation to harmless feminine interests.

"Thank heaven," said Jacintha, "whoever packed for this trip put in my pincushions, even if they did leave out my photographs. Brian. My children . . ."

"What could you possibly want with photographs of people who are still alive?"

As they chatted and Jacintha completed her toilet, the maid brought in the lunch basket. Though it was light, they each took a handle and carried it between them.

"Do we lock the door?" inquired Jacintha.

"No one ever locks a door here. Anyway, it's so easy to replace something if it should be stolen. One can spend hours every day shopping for new things." Cherry gave a little laugh. "Lovemaking grows tiresome here, but no one *ever* gives up shopping."

Jacintha laughed too and then suddenly sobered. "How dreadful."

Cherry disagreed as they walked briskly along the hall, not dawdling as they had last evening. "It's most fortunate, actually. There's so little else to do."

"But there must be *something* one can find to do!"

"You can do whatever you like, of course. There are no rules or regulations."

"That seems considerate."

"It may seem considerate—for a year or two. But

eventually, you'll find that since there is nothing you *must* do, there is nothing you will want to do." Cherry stopped before a heavy carved door. "We don't realize," she said, "how greatly we depend on our duties."

It took both of them, pulling very hard, to get the door open. And then they were squinting into a day so brilliantly clear and blue that they had to pause a moment and shade their eyes, immediately snapping their parasols open. They had emerged on the other side of the great entrance, which gave them an entirely different view of the countryside.

A thick, untrimmed green lawn, filled with blue and yellow wildflowers, sloped away beneath them. They heard a hissing sound as a great cloud of sulfur-laden steam blew into the air and wafted toward them. They held their noses and grimaced.

"This place smells to high heaven," said Jacintha.

"That's what he intended."

They both burst out laughing, as if at the greatest witticism. Jacintha had begun to realize how precious laughter was here, and they agreed to laugh at everything that could, in any possible sense, be construed as funny.

The rushing, swishing sound died away, the steam disappeared, and the air was fresh and clean and exhilarating.

Whatever this place was, it had many charms and great beauty. She and Cherry should be able to spend a long time exploring its possibilities—months, perhaps years—and then her imagination stopped, for she had been struck by a black horror. Even if they spent one hundred years, or two hundred, they would have nothing at all to whittle away the eternity confronting them. No matter how long they spent at any project, they could do nothing to lessen the time. There was no goal, no limit.

Although the steam cloud had blown away and the air had cleared, Jacintha felt dizzy and anxious.

"Isn't it incredible," she whispered, eager to escape her own thoughts. "The mountains in the distance, the boiling caldrons, the sulfur and brimstone, everything as I expected and yet so entirely different. And the air! It's more delicious than anything I've ever smelled."

"Yes," agreed Cherry. "Living the way we did, like plants in a conservatory, all but immobilized—" She gave a quick little shudder, as if the recollection disgusted her. "You get simply *wild* for something primitive."

They strolled down the sloping lawn and made their way across the high, thick, wet grass, dragging their long skirts, chatting idly and contentedly, and from time to time bursting into exclamations of delightful laughter.

The sun passed to and fro among the clouds, brilliant one moment and hidden the next. In the distance they could see that other men and women were out today, too, though there were fewer than might have been expected from the size of the lodge.

They circled a shallow, steaming lake of brilliant smeared orange and rusty water, and Jacintha pointed with pleased wonder at the clumps of grass growing in the hot liquid. They passed great craters filled with boiling water, one of them pouring forth a stream two hundred feet wide which meandered over white graveled earth, trickling and bubbling and reeking of sulfur so that they daintily held their noses as they neared its rim.

They rounded a corner of the lodge and came upon a long line of carriages, the drivers lounging or wandering about or gossiping. Cherry explained that the coaches were available at all hours, at a moment's notice, ready to drive wherever one decided to go.

A gentleman elegantly dressed in English tweeds was wrapping a beautiful young lady in a heavily embroidered carriage robe. Now he sprang into the open vehicle and they were off with a smart snapping of the whip and clattering of hooves.

Jacintha and Cherry watched them, standing quietly to one side, both their faces still and wistful.

"Some women," said Jacintha finally, "seem to make happy matches here."

Cherry shook her head. "It won't last. It looks very pretty today in the sunshine. But by tomorrow afternoon they may detest each other. Disappointments—especially those of the senses—are felt more keenly here."

The carriage they chose was a fine one, open on all sides, a small phaeton intended for two occupants. It was shiny black with red and yellow decorations, and four black horses stood ready to draw it. Jacintha looked at the coachman somewhat anxiously, afraid it would be Grant, who she feared might have been delegated her tormentor. But it was not. It was only some nondescript individual, though he wore splendid livery. With great deference, he handed first Cherry and then Jacintha into the carriage and spread a handsome robe, embroidered with flowers and birds, across their laps.

The two women looked at each other with gleeful smiles, settling into their corners, making themselves feel cozy and pampered and prepared for a delightful excursion.

The coachman was waiting for their order. "Where shall we go?" asked Cherry.

"Heavens, I don't know. I haven't the slightest idea. You tell him."

"I've seen so little of this place. Take the north road," she instructed him. "We will guide you as we go along. Isn't this better than walking? You see how free we are?"

The coachman snapped his whip above the horses' backs, the carriage gave a quick lurch, and they were away at that same bewildering speed with which Grant had careened her through the forests and over the fields yesterday.

Yesterday?

Don't think about how long it has been or what has happened. Think only of this minute.

"How enchanting!" cried Jacintha. "I've never enjoyed anything so much. Do you remember how you used to take me driving on Sunday afternoons when we went to visit Grandfather Anson?"

"Of course I do. If you could have seen yourself, Jacintha, with your pretty ruffled dresses and long black curls and sweet manners. Even at five you were a perfect little lady.''

They laughed at that, for obviously she had been less a lady than she had seemed, and so had her mother. But it was even more humorous that Cherry should speak of how she had looked at the age of five, as here they were twenty years later at exactly the same age.

They went bouncing over the meadows, lurching in the deep ruts left by other carriages, through small forests, along the edges of low, pine-covered hills, through steam clouds rolling off boiling ponds, gray-blue and orange. They stared in wonder and craned their necks to look back. Everywhere the colors were intense, but also soft and misted, giving the miraculous effect of reality combined with hallucination.

At the foot of a rock-piled mountain, they passed a little lake covered with bright yellow water lilies floating among the pads. They saw deer and a number of elk. There were also several iron deer and dogs, painted chocolate brown, exactly like those that stood on the lawns at home.

Over and over they exclaimed at the beauty of this place, its mystical unreality and the clear, bright air that gave the illusion that it was possible to see infinity. From time to time a vast cloud of floating, whirling blue steam, outlined in brilliant yellow, would pass across their vision and they would find themselves enveloped in its thick, sulfurous vapors.

Occasionally they saw Indians.

Cherry said that they were merely passing through the

place on one of their transmigrations. They did some hunting and fishing, and their host frequently joined in, for he liked their company, their fine physical hardihood, and their freedom from the attitudes of his other guests. They never stayed long, but there were always a few of them about.

"I thought he was an Indian when I . . ." began Jacintha and stopped abruptly.

Cherry patted her arm reassuringly. "Never mind, darling. We can't avoid him entirely, of course. It's only that I think we should avoid him when we can."

"I intend to avoid him entirely!"

Cherry glanced at her and smiled. "You can only avoid him when he is willing for you to. Do you honestly imagine that if we were to round this corner and find him there, you would be able to ignore him? Remember, he offers the only hope there is in this crowded, desolate place."

"He offers the wrong kind of hope for me!" cried Jacintha, with a strange, eager anger.

"I wonder if you know," began Cherry slowly, watching her as she spoke, "that you are exactly the kind of woman he finds most appealing?"

She was so stunned by this, particularly by the fact that it was Cherry who had said it, that she felt as if she were strangling. She stared back in pain and confusion.

"I don't know what you mean," Jacintha replied in a scarcely audible voice.

"I mean what I said."

Jacintha glanced stealthily toward her and found Cherry's eyes fixed with a look of bright, watchful curiosity. There was no tenderness or softness, but only the suspicion and malice of a mistrustful animal. Jacintha wanted to leap from the coach and run. Then Cherry's expression softened.

I must have been mistaken, thought Jacintha, still looking at her with helpless fascination.

Cherry continued, "You are proud and thoughtful and take things more seriously than they ever deserve. He has great sport amusing himself with women like you, for you are always more ready to be his victim than any other kind."

Jacintha felt humiliated by Cherry's words. She was overcome with confusion. She could not believe that Cherry would be so willfully cruel.

Then he was not attracted to her beauty or charm—but only by her susceptibility to pain? She was not a woman to be cherished, but rather prey, to be played with—even molested—at whim?

This was what Cherry was telling her, but Jacintha could not accept it. Surely he was not like that. Or even if he was, he would not be like that with her. The women he had amused himself with had lacked her qualities.

Last night, certainly, there had been no hint that he could ever do her harm. His tenderness had surpassed any she had ever known. His passion, though urgent and unbridled, had given her voluptuous pleasure beyond imagining.

Did he intend to torment her, after all?

Cherry wanted to frighten her, since she must fear that Jacintha had become as much his willing subject as she was herself.

To Jacintha's surprise, a quick spasm of reminiscent pleasure spread throughout her body, filling and expanding her breasts, making them glow and tingle. And with extraordinary clarity she recalled his commanding beauty, the power and sensuality stunning her senses, immobilizing her self-control.

The sensation was so pleasurable that she paused, scarcely breathing, her eyes wide and sparkling.

How did that happen? How did he catch me off guard?

And, feeling her face and throat burn with guilty embarrassment, she cast Cherry a hasty glance, to see if she had been observed. But Cherry, by the greatest good luck, was looking the other way.

She wished she had not found so many reasons to give him up. For the truth was, she found herself obsessed by a newfound sensual appetite. Her love for Cherry was greater than her love of herself, but still . . .

Cherry's head turned and she smiled quickly and innocently at Jacintha.

"I only mention these things, darling, so that you may protect yourself."

Jacintha hung her head again and looked both shamed and grateful. "Thank you," she murmured.

They were driving along at the same merry clip, when

suddenly Cherry cried, "Oh, look where we are! Have you ever seen anything so picturesque? Stop here, driver. We want to get out."

She flung aside the carriage robe and climbed down. Jacintha followed and they stood together beside the coach, staring with wonder at the magnificent vista spread before them.

They were on a high cliff, overlooking a vast cascade of empty, steaming white terraces, descending, one after the other, away into the far distance. A few dwarfed and warped pines were stuck about like artificial trees in a stage set, and there were some odd roots thrusting up from the chalky white earth. Other trees, stripped bare, were the color and texture of driftwood, and their branches twisted wildly about the trunks as if they had been caught and petrified by writhing rage. The sun was hot and so intensely brilliant that it brought tears to their eyes. The ominous scene itself was both dismal and awe inspiring. Though it may have been, as Cherry said, "picturesque," it was also alien and ugly, and Jacintha could not look at it.

"It's hideous," Jacintha said, shaking her head. "There's something evil in it."

"Suppose there is?" asked Cherry lightly. "Evil is not without purpose."

Jacintha did not believe that such a remark was sincere; Cherry must have made it for some other reason. Cherry had not forgiven her, that was plain enough. It would take a great deal of time, and infinite patience, before Cherry would trust her again.

Jacintha turned away and began to stroll toward the edge of a forest that lay on the far side of the blazing white plateau. Dejected and unhappy, she did not notice Cherry following thoughtfully behind and was startled by her clear, light voice.

"Your first love is not always the one you thought it was, is it?"

Jacintha turned and they stood face to face. "For instance," Cherry continued, "you probably thought that Brian was the first man you loved."

"Of course he was," replied Jacintha, trying to sound more confident than she felt. "I never loved Martin. I never even imagined that I did. I was a dutiful wife to him—until I met Brian—but I never loved any man before Brian."

"You never loved Brian either."

They confronted each other, two small figures against the harsh, glittering white floor of the terrace. Their silhouettes looked exaggeratedly female, breasts and hips accentuated by their corsets, their skirts trailing behind them in the dry dust. They twirled their ruffled parasols, spinning them like pinwheels as they balanced them lightly on their shoulders.

"Don't you see what's happened?" asked Cherry reasonably.

"Of course I don't see what's happened," retorted Jacintha.

Cherry laughed, half stifling the sound with her gloved palm, as if amusement at someone else's expense were impolite. "But, my dear child—don't you see now that you were *never* in love before? That you fell in love for the first time when you looked around on Roaring Mountain and saw him standing there?"

Jacintha started to answer but could not speak. Her eyes were full and her chin was quivering. She turned and went on, convinced that something in this wicked landscape had infected Cherry, hoping that if she could lure her to the forest, its cool cleanness would restore her innocence and mercy.

Cherry, however, caught up with her, slipped one arm about her waist, and spoke in a soft, confiding tone: "Darling—don't be distressed. My, my, how sensitive you are. If I hurt your feelings, I'm sorry, I apologize."

Jacintha brightened at this and turned to Cherry. "I *don't* love him," she said with intense earnestness. "You must believe me. I *don't* love him."

Cherry gazed into her face a moment longer, carefully searching Jacintha's expression for uncontrollable flickers that might betray her. Then, seemingly satisfied, she drew her toward the forest.

"For your sake, Jacintha, I hope you never will."

They had come to the edge of the dark, fragrant woods and, as they paused, gazing into its mossy depths, they could hear the old trees creaking like rocking chairs. Clumps of bright blue flowers sprang energetically around a little pool, so clear that the skeeters darting about its surface cast their dotted shadows on the sandy bottom.

Jacintha wanted to ask why, but knew she must not.

That was Cherry's secret and she must never try to discover it. Now, hearing a strange, unexpected sound, she raised her head.

"What can that be?"

"I don't know," said Cherry. "Let's find out."

"Perhaps it's dangerous."

"It won't be. And, if it is, danger is one of the few antidotes to the interminable boredom of this place."

The forest curved away abruptly, and they saw a crater the size of a small lake, filled with boiling, ugly, gray mud. It was hideous, and they stared in fascinated awe and revulsion.

"How horrible," said Jacintha.

"I wonder how deep it is?" mused Cherry.

Jacintha gave an involuntary backward start. "Don't even think of that! It must be bottomless."

"Look—there's another lake of boiling mud."

"I don't want to see anymore!"

Cherry turned and surveyed her with delicate, surprised amusement. "Why, Jacintha—where's your curiosity? Come along. Seeing it can't hurt you."

The air was so thick with choking sulfurous fumes that they began to cough. At Cherry's insistence they skirted the crater, half obscured by swirling mists, and advanced with slow, careful steps toward a low hillside.

There, at its base, they saw a great cavern, like an open wound in the earth, and from it came an arching torrent of gray mud rushing forth in an angry turmoil. Rumbling and hissing, sending up vast, enveloping clouds

of steam, brawling, raging, it rolled and heaved, splatter-
ing in all directions.

This natural phenomenon was a sure indication of his
presence in the vicinity. Tumultuous and devastating, it
must be part of his general scheme for evil.

Jacintha stared at it in horror, imagining that if
anything fell into this crater it would be swept down into
the nether region. For this, she felt, was part of its core,
like oozing pus reaching the skin from an internal wound;
this terror and rage and ugliness was what the earth's crust
hid from view.

Involuntarily she was retreating from it, taking small,
uncertain backward, steps, while Cherry made her way
slowly forward, approaching that monstrous, molten mass.

The clouds of sulfur were so thick that it was like
struggling in a gale of endless veils of chiffon. The fumes
clawed at their throats and lungs so that they coughed
constantly and helplessly.

Suddenly, awakening from her stunned silence, Jacintha screamed and rushed forward. She grabbed Cherry by
one arm and began to drag her back. Cherry resisted, and
Jacintha pulled harder and harder, with all her strength.
All at once Cherry stopped so abruptly that both of them
staggered backward.

"What's the matter, Jacintha?"

They stood face to face again, coughing and rubbing
their burning eyes.

"You'll be killed!"

"Dear one, how could I *possibly* be killed?"

Jacintha realized with unbelieving shock that Cherry had spoken to her angrily and was shaking herself free with such energy and disdain that Jacintha let go.

"Don't do that again," she warned. "*I'm* going to explore. You can come along or not."

Cherry slowly started forward again.

While Jacintha watched, Cherry moved nearer and nearer to the terrible boiling crater. "Oh, Cherry," she was murmuring. "Come back, please come back, please come back...."

But Cherry ignored her and, with sudden determination, Jacintha started forward again, reaching Cherry and gently taking her hand. Cherry turned her head and smiled. Jacintha felt she had been rewarded.

Together, carefully and experimentally, they moved nearer and nearer to the crater's edge. They grasped each other's hands so hard that their knuckles turned white. Their faces were moist and shiny and their clothes stuck to them, wet from their perspiring bodies and the stinking steam. At any moment the ground could break through like a piecrust. Any step they took might be the last one. The nearer they approached, the greater the danger became.

Since they could not be killed again, were they destined to spend eternity bobbing about in that boiling mud? Cherry must have gone mad to insist on taking such a chance.

But Jacintha loyally took step for step with her.

She could not hang back, not for fear of showing her cowardice but for the vivid sense of how intolerable it would be to remain here if Cherry should be swept into the crater. If it was to happen, it must happen to both of them.

At last they came within five or six feet of the edge. They stood transfixed for several moments, speechless. Jacintha grew aware of that sense of distance from herself that always came just as she was about to faint.

She gave a timid little tug at Cherry's hand and a look of humble pleading filled her eyes. Cherry, apparently not seeing her white, sickened face, stared back blankly.

"Isn't it exciting!" Cherry demanded. "Look!" And she leaned forward.

Jacintha felt her head whirl. "I—"she whispered. "I—"

But Jacintha could not speak. Time seemed to stretch endlessly, and it seemed she felt herself bending obediently forward.

Then Cherry let go of her hand and Jacintha flailed out, searching desperately for support, feeling a gentle push at her back. Her arms flung wide. She gave a wailing, lonely scream and began pitching forward, sailing in slow motion into the yawning mouth of the crater, like a great bird.

Tumbling, as if she had been struck a violent blow, she felt herself seized and flung furiously back. The next instant she and Cherry lay on the chalk-white earth, locked in each other's arms—wet, panting, and sobbing in a strange, hard, tearless way that was like coughing.

Jacintha lay on her back, her arms around Cherry, staring up at the sun that appeared through the steam like a flat orange circle. She seemed to be coming back from a distant journey as she glided smoothly, swiftly, in silence, sweeping nearer and nearer to the center of a swirling spiral, suddenly regaining consciousness.

What was it that happened?

Cherry wanted me to fall into the crater. She wanted to be rid of me forever—out of her sight, out of her heart. She knew that I was fainting and so she let go of my hand, and . . .

No! She did not!

It was Cherry who saved me.

If Cherry had not thrown her arms around me and flung us back, if she had not risked herself, I would have fallen into the boiling mud and been swept away.

That is what happened, and that is what I must remember.

She felt Cherry stir beside her and then, moving very slowly, as if every muscle were stiff, Cherry sat up. Jacintha lay a moment, looking at her. Cherry was still coughing. Her hat had been knocked to one side, and her hair was dusted with white powdery earth. The white earth had made pasty smudges on her face. Her gown was tangled and twisted and so laden with white dust that the bright plaid looked dim and dingy. Even her lashes bore a sprinkling of white powder.

She was busy trying to put herself in order, patting and twitching, tugging and brushing, like a sparrow in a dust bath, so preoccupied that it was a few seconds before she looked directly at Jacintha.

A dazed, questioning look passed between them.

There was a tense feeling of anxiety—something was about to happen.

With a tremendous rush of air and clattering of hooves, he arrived on his black stallion and sat a moment, a cloud of white dust shifting around him, partially obscured by the restless, hovering vapors.

Then he swung down abruptly and reached his hand toward Cherry, who extended her own and was whisked to her feet. Next he drew Jacintha up, lightly and swiftly, and all three stood looking at one another.

Today he wore the fringed and beaded leggings of the Blackfoot nation, a tribe believed to have got its name by roaming through regions destroyed by fire. His chest and shoulders were naked, brown and shining, and his black hair was ruffled by the wind. He wore beaded moccasins, but no headdress. His fists were on his hips and his white teeth shone in a strange half-smile that instantly made them wary. He was, quite clearly, in full possession of that alluring magnificence and unbridled power that had exerted such malefic influence upon them.

"What happened here?" he demanded. "An accident?"

Quickly, as if at a prearranged signal, both women opened their handbags and took out mirrors, peering into them, and began setting their bonnets straight, wiping their faces with embroidered white handkerchiefs, tucking wisps of hair back into place. They frowned and pursed their lips and appeared to be engrossed by this activity.

All at once he threw back his head and laughed, a hearty, ribald laugh which was an insult to them both.

They stopped, handbags still held open, arrested in gestures of rearranging themselves, and looked at him in openmouthed surprise and anger.

"Well," he said at last. "Which of you is the guilty one? I can't tell by looking at you. Either one of you could have done it."

Jacintha promptly turned her back and stood tapping her foot and staring toward the forest, where his horse had wandered off in search of water and grass.

Their parasols had been flung away, and the sun beat down with a steady insistence that made Jacintha's blood throb and leap just under the surface of her skin.

The smashing and rumbling of the caldron filled the air. Sulfur fumes steamed continuously about them. The heat was fierce and smothering.

Cherry burst into another coughing spell. "Guilty of what?" she demanded, hacking so hard she could scarcely speak.

"Don't play with me," he advised. "One of you tried to throw the other into that thing over there."

Jacintha shuddered to hear him call it "that thing," as if it were alive, for her own terror and imagination had made it a kind of subterranean monster, thrusting its head and mouth out of the earth in search of prey.

"Which was it? Jacintha?"

And he gave her an impertinent whack on the bottom, knocking a cloud of dust from her skirts. She jumped and reached back with both hands, but did not cry out.

"Come," he said, taking hold of Jacintha's shoulder

to turn her around, and sliding one arm about each of their waists. "Let's get out of this infernal muck." The three of them started toward the forest.

The oppressive fumes cleared, although streamers of the smell wandered after them for some distance. Presently they stopped coughing and rubbing their eyes. Suddenly free, as if imprisoned back there against their wills, it now seemed they had stayed an interminable time and been unable to escape until he came to rescue them.

"You always arrive," said Cherry, as they walked along, "at the most inconvenient times."

"Oh?" he asked, and his tone was full of mocking amusement. "Then it *was* you."

Cherry whirled about. She stamped her foot and fiercely clenched her fists. "How dare you make such a filthy accusation!"

"You mean it was Jacintha?" He had a pleased, lazy smile on his face and looked from one to the other.

"No!" cried Cherry. "It was *not* Jacintha! It wasn't either of us! It was you!"

"What are you trying to do?" Jacintha demanded furiously. "Are you trying to make me believe that my mother meant to push me into that crater? Are you trying to make us hate each other for your entertainment?"

He glanced at her briefly, started to turn his attention to Cherry, and then, as if caught by something in her expression, gave her a long, steady stare, curious and amused. "Are you possibly naïve enough to believe that was not her intention?"

They stood there now, close to the forest. There were a few ravens in the sky. His great black stallion chomped on the grass. The air was still, and a wonderful peace settled over the woods. Small sounds of birds and crackling twigs mingled with the faint rumblings of the caldron.

Jacintha stared back at him, proud and defiant, but his expression did not alter. He continued to look at her as if this situation was comical in a way both she and Cherry should have been able to appreciate. He even seemed to pity them for their lack of humor.

Then she turned quickly to Cherry. "Don't you see what he's trying to do? If he can find something to make him laugh, what happens to *us* doesn't concern him at all."

Cherry watched her as she talked, squinting her eyes a little because of the sun, but Jacintha could see the sorrow and pain in their depths. Slowly she nodded.

"I know," she murmured. "Of course."

With her back to him, Jacintha took hold of Cherry's hands and spoke in a low, intense voice: "I don't *want* to know if that was what you meant to happen to me. It doesn't matter because you saved me. Cherry—we must not let him trick us into abandoning each other."

Cherry lowered her eyes.

Jacintha gazed eagerly into Cherry's averted face. His heavily muscled arms crossed upon his naked chest, he continued to watch them with mild interest, as if this were a performance staged for his benefit. Finally, Cherry kissed Jacintha's cheek, and they began to walk again along the forest's edge, until—still silent—they reached the blazing white floor of the upper terrace. Straight ahead in the distance stood the phaeton with the driver in place, a small silhouette against the horizon. The sight of it was a shock, like returning from a long, hazardous journey to find that during all the years of absence no single piece of furniture has been moved in one's parlor.

Here, as if by mutual consent, they stopped again. Cherry put her arms about Jacintha and held her tenderly. Tears came into their eyes and spilled down their faces.

After a moment he casually remarked:

"If you would forgive your enemy, first do him a wrong. It's an old saying. I've forgotten whose."

Both women looked at him, still holding each other for assurance and support. The sun threw sharp, dark shadows over his face, and his beauty seemed intolerable, a bitter, mocking challenge; they held each other closer than ever.

"Why do you want to hurt us?" asked Jacintha, her voice wistful and plaintive.

He smiled. "I don't want to hurt you," he said. "If you are hurt by what happens here, that is your own choice."

There was a moment's silence, and then he continued. "You want to have me be a part of your world, the kind of man you always knew—one who pitied women and feared them. I don't and can't. Women are, along with hunting and fishing and gambling, my chief diversion. I regard them neither with contempt nor with awe,

and that's the mixture you're accustomed to. There is no
hypocrisy in my feelings toward you, and I think it's that
attitude that you hold against me. You want me to take
your jealousy seriously and be considerate of you for
allowing yourselves to be dominated by an artificial emotion. I am not in sympathy with such nonsense. If you will
be jealous, and it is not as inevitable as you both believe,
then I decline any responsibility for your pangs."

He smiled, first at Cherry and then at Jacintha.

"You are two extraordinarily beautiful and desirable
women. It would not do me much credit if I avoided either
one of you. Would it?"

Jacintha saw that beguiling, treacherous tenderness
come into his eyes, an expression infinitely more dangerous than his anger.

She grasped Cherry's hand. "Quick! Let's get away
from here before something happens."

Cherry jerked free and turned on Jacintha with a look
of excited anger.

"What are you talking about, Jacintha? We can't run
away from him! We're in his country. There's no place we
can escape to. Running won't solve this." She looked up
at him once more. "You don't want to hurt us, but you
don't care if we get hurt. Of course. I knew that. I've
known you for some time now ... haven't I?"

"Yes. You have." He smiled, and then laughed
softly. "We have," he amended.

He and Cherry were looking into each other's eyes,
laughing. It was not a loud, boisterous sound, which

Jacintha could have scorned, but a soft, conspiratorial chuckle, which made her feel as lost and cold as if she had wakened alone in a dark, strange room. She grew more and more frantic, wondering what she could do or say to break this bond, to destroy whatever secret they shared, and to attract his attention back to her.

"You're a liar!" cried Jacintha.

That stopped their laughter and they turned toward her suddenly, with such a complete erasure of humor from their faces that she began a slow, involuntary retreat. Then, overcome with a strangling terror so great that she had to do something to release the tension, she picked up her skirts and began to run.

She ran blindly, stumbling along in her high heels, her purple silk legs flashing back and forth. Followed by a little cloud of white dust that seemed to scurry after her across the blistered plateau, she vanished from their sight, a pale blue-and-purple figure, growing smaller, disappearing toward the bright wide-open sky.

She concentrated fiercely on those things directly before her eyes—the dead white blazing earth, the boiling puddles of gray mud, the hovering vapors—on anything but the memory of their smiles, sharing something she did not know, mocking her and making her feel ridiculous.

In the distance, she heard them begin to laugh. His voice first, loud and hearty, turning everything human into sham and pretense. And, following along, weaving in upon it like a tender, lighter melody, came Cherry's response.

Jacintha started to turn, but she could not face them. Their laughter swelled like an orchestra, filling the air with its sound, and she ran on, sobbing. Jacintha had run so far and so hard that she began to gasp and her lungs felt raw and burning. The blood pounded in her ears, roaring louder and louder, until it finally drowned out the sound of their mirth.

At last, staggering, no longer able to run, she reached the coach and stood leaning against one of its yellow wheels, her chest heaving and swelling, one hand pressed to the stabbing pain in her side.

The coachman sat on his roost. He glanced at her with cold disinterest, then turned back to wait.

After some minutes, Jacintha surreptitiously began to look for them. First she peered toward the forest. Then she searched the upward slope, beyond the edge of where the terraces descended. There was nothing in sight, in any direction, but the sick white earth, the blue sky, and the wall of black-green mountains.

What a fool I was!

I turned, like a coward, and ran away.

How they must both despise me!

And now they are alone together somewhere. I accomplished the thing I most wanted to avoid.

Thereupon, she heard a piercing whistle that seemed to come from some distance yet sounded so sharp and near that she covered her ears with her hands, wincing.

The next moment there was a drumming of hoofbeats and his black stallion appeared, far ahead, galloping toward the horizon. They rose into view, walking up over the crest of the terrace, two figures looking very small from this distance.

Jacintha saw him lift Cherry swiftly onto the horse, swinging himself up behind her. Then the great animal wheeled off at a gallop, rounding the edge of the terraces, plunging downward, and disappearing into the landscape.

She had been so absorbed in watching them that she was not aware she had begun to cry. She saw a tear splash into the white dust at her feet and dashed away the next with her gloved hand. With a melancholy sigh, she gathered her heavy, dust-covered skirts and climbed into the phaeton.

"Take me to the main lodge," she called out, and immediately the coachman cracked his whip, the horses leaped forward like jackrabbits, and the small coach started bouncing and joggling along.

Jacintha opened her bag and looked at herself in the mirror, gravely shaking her head. Her hair hung in damp strings. Her face was flushed from the sun and smudged with white dust, and her body, inside the heavy cocoon of corset and petticoats and thick, ruffled skirt, smelled of sweat. Chagrined and angry at being in such a state of disarray, she wanted to weep. Finally, disgusted, she dropped the mirror back into her bag and sat holding onto the side of the coach.

She noticed that it had grown colder and drew the lap robe across her knees. Then, looking up, she found that while she had been absorbed in repairing herself, the blue had faded from the sky, and clouds had rolled across it, gray and stormy and shaggy. The trees whipped smartly about, bending and twisting like dancers limbering up.

Jacintha shivered and put one hand to her throat to fasten her collar. There was a quick spasm of light. She drew the robe closer, snuggling into it, trying to curl deeper into herself as well.

It's going to storm!

Her eyes opened wide; she sat up straight and began turning frantically in every direction, looking out both sides of the coach, with no idea of what she hoped to find. The coachman was lashing the horses, urging them on faster and faster.

"Stop!" she yelled at him. He paid no attention. She called again, louder, and just as she opened her mouth, the thunder rattled. She shouted again and again, but he did not so much as turn his head. "It's going to rain!" she cried. "I'll be soaked!" On he drove, bounding across the meadows, through the ragged little forests, over the rutted dirt roads. He plowed his way through fields of wildflowers, splashing through sulfur streams and tearing past vaporous, boiling blue pools.

Finally, furious at her inability to make him obey, she gave up and sank back in her seat. The sky was flickering now, dark one instant and flaring brilliantly the next. The thunder came rolling out of the mountains. Jacintha, her hands clenched tightly together, winced as if she had been struck with each new flash of lightning and report of thunder.

It will stop. It won't storm. It's only threatening.

I can't stand it if it storms!
Oh, he's horrible—horrible!

Jacintha could see them together with hallucinatory vividness: Cherry's eager face turned toward his; his big, square-fingered hands pressing her belly and breasts; his mouth close to hers. Jacintha could feel within her own body their excitement, growing swifter and stronger and more demanding every instant; their urgent need for each other. And now, as the thunder roared like a voice in universal rage, she wailed and closed her eyes, putting her hands over her ears and crouching on the edge of her seat.

She felt something wet strike her cheek, and the rain came splatting down.

"Oh, no!" she howled in futile, lonely protest.

Her little carriage rushed along, faster than ever, the driver beating the horses in a kind of insane frenzy. The rain increased so suddenly that it was as if she had stepped under a waterfall. The sky was lit with such great white flashes that it seemed the world must be exploding; each stroke accompanied by a burst and roar of thunder.

Jacintha began to cry again. Soon she was moaning and sobbing piteously. Like an animal seeking shelter, she crept down onto the floor of the carriage, doubled up, beating her fists on the floor in the darkness. She pulled the blanket over her head and was buried within it.

Her mother had deserted her, gone off with him and was now advertising, for all who could hear, their ardent lovemaking.

She was filled with hatred. Crouching in darkness

with neither air nor light, jolted and tossed by the rocking coach, she sobbed herself into exhaustion.

And then, while the storm still snarled and crashed all around, the carriage stopped short.

Jacintha turned back an edge of the blanket and saw that they had arrived in front of the lodge. With a gasp of horror she saw that people were standing there, dozens of them, hundreds perhaps, talking and laughing together, sheltered from the storm under the vast porch roof. At each appalling crash of thunder they pointed, jumped, and burst into excited laughter.

Swiftly she flung off the blanket and sat back on the seat once more, feeling her skirt instantly soak through. Some of them had seen her. Two or three men were watching her with amusement; she lifted her chin high and stared at them haughtily. Then, after looking about for her hat, she decided it had been lost along the way, picked up her wet skirts, and started to climb down.

Two of the men, broadly smiling, sprang forward with offers of help. Jacintha refused to extend her hand and got down unassisted, though with difficulty.

Her clothing was so wet that it dripped and stuck fast to her body. The ruffles and layers of her petticoats clung, soggy and heavy, to her legs as she moved. Her hair was smeared across her forehead and neck in an unsightly bunch. Feeling herself ugly, betrayed in every way, she ducked her head and shaded her eyes, making her way through the crowd as swiftly as she could.

In the lobby there was the usual acre or more of

luggage waiting to be distributed, lackeys running about, Indians wrapped in blankets, some of them smoking pipes, others squatting on the floor playing dice, and numbers of well-dressed, good-looking men and women.

Jacintha pushed her way through the throng, hoping desperately that they would not notice her. But she could not help darting a look out of the corner of her eye and seeing people observing her with expressions of surprise, amusement, boredom, even outrage that such a bedraggled creature should be among them. She felt that it took her at least an hour to cross the lobby, and when at last she gained the hallway she started down it with tremendous relief, heading as fast as she could go for her own room, seclusion, obscurity, and, she hoped, forgetfulness.

But she could not escape the storm.

She could hear it still rolling and grumbling and banging in the atmosphere outside. As she passed windows she saw the lightning break again and again, and the rain came down with shattering force. Shaking her head, whimpering, she ran on and on, down one corridor and then another. At last she reached her room, flung open the door and rushed in, slammed it shut and leaned back against it, panting, still crying, still shaking her head from side to side.

The experience had been more torturesome than those few minutes before Martin had leveled his gun at her.

Now, as she leaned against the door, she could see the lightning through the windows, and she rushed to draw the heavy draperies. Though she paced the room with her hands over her ears, she could not shut out the swelling sound of thunder that shook the room with its force. Engrossed in her own violent participation in the storm, her hatred of Cherry, her wild fury against him, she jumped with a shriek when the door was thrown open suddenly.

Jacintha had not lighted a lamp and the room was in darkness. A woman's figure stood silhouetted in the doorway.

"Who are you?" she cried.

There was a moment's silence while Jacintha stared at the intruder, so terrified that her breath had stopped.

"I am your maid, madam," came the timid, quiet reply. "May I come in?"

"Oh!" Jacintha let out a sigh of relief.

She had thought, for a moment, that it was Cherry. To confront Cherry now would be the most terrifying experience she could contemplate. No matter what she had to do, that must never happen.

"Shall I light the lamp, madam?"

Jacintha sighed. "Yes, you may as well."

There was a soft, scratching sound and the next moment the big glass-shaded lamp on the center table flowered into a radiant glow. Then, seeing how the maid stood staring at her, Jacintha, after a moment's puzzlement, looked down at her soaked dress and caught sight of herself in the mirror. Her hair was strung out of the combs and hung wet and sodden upon her cheeks and neck, sticking fast to the bodice of her gown. Water dripped off the sleeves and skirt, and she could feel it running down her legs. She shuddered.

"Madam, you'll take a chill. Can't I build a fire and help you undress?"

"Yes," agreed Jacintha, grateful now for the companionship and for someone to help her with all the trivial things she had never done for herself. "Please do. What is your name?"

"Beth, madam."

Beth was busy setting the fire, and presently it was going well. "Come here now, madam, and let me undress you before this nice warm blaze."

Jacintha walked slowly to the fire, turning her back so that Beth could unhook her gown.

The room was more cheerful now with the leaping fire and, when she had removed Jacintha's clothing and rubbed her skin dry, Beth brought a dressing gown and held it for her to slip into. Jacintha sat in a chair, warming herself, and closed her eyes while Beth took the pins and combs from her hair, dried it as well as she could with a towel, and began to brush it.

The stroking along her scalp was so soothing that presently, despite the incessant roar of the storm outside and the bursting thunder which was sometimes so violent that it seemed the building itself must be cracking open, she began to have a luxurious sense of ease and pleasant drowsiness. She moved her head against the brushstrokes, like a kitten being petted. This room was so warm and softly lighted, so beautifully furnished, so complete a nest, as it were, that she did not care about him or about Cherry or about anything else but this exquisite, delightful comfort.

"I love it here," she said finally.

She glanced up at Beth, who was bending over her. Beth was a few years older than she, and though she was pleasant in appearance and her face looked kindly, if somewhat stupid, she looked too common to be considered pretty.

Beth was shocked. "You *love* it here?"

"In this room, I mean."

"Oh, yes, the room," agreed Beth, as if relieved to have found that her mistress was not entirely mad. She was twining the ends of Jacintha's hair carefully about her fingers now and brushing them, while still slightly damp, into long loose curls that hung almost to her waist. "The rooms are very handsome."

"So is the out-of-doors. For him—it is all perfect."

"For him, yes. But for no one else, madam. For no one else, believe me. I have been here a long while."

"You have?" Jacintha turned, gesturing that she could stop the brushing now. "How long have you been here?"

"Well, I don't recall how many years it's been. It's too many for me to add. But I remember when I died. It was March twelfth, 1643. I was burned for a witch, madam."

"Burned for a witch!" whispered Jacintha. Her

brown eyes opened wide. "*Were* you one?"

Beth gave a low chuckle. "No, madam. I was not. They said I'd had intercourse with the Devil. And the humor of it all is, madam, that I had not had intercourse with him then, nor have I at any time since I got here."

Jacintha blinked at that and then, suddenly, they both laughed. They laughed delightedly at the joke on Beth and, through the shared mirth, came to feel very friendly toward each other.

"Has he asked you?" inquired Jacintha.

"Never, madam. Not while I lived and not since I died, even though I died, as it were, for his sake."

Jacintha shook her head and got up. "It's like him. Do you think he ever will?"

"Never, madam. Or he would not have put me to this kind of work. Look at the difference between us. I'm not pretty enough for him. He likes a woman like you . . . or like Mrs. Anson, in the next room."

Beth nodded toward the wall. Jacintha felt her heart knot, as if someone had squeezed it. She walked to the window, drew back the drapery just enough to peek out, and saw that the storm was almost over. Light flashed across the sky far in the distance as if bidding them farewell, fluttering a negligent sign as it disappeared across the mountains. The thunder gave a last, surly mutter, and the rain was a mere spatter and trickle. Jacintha let the drapery fall and turned back to Beth.

"He likes Mrs. Anson, you say?" she asked, with elaborate unconcern.

Jacintha walked to the dressing table, seated herself on the fringed and padded taboret, and began to dust a light film of powder over her face. She leaned forward to look at herself, smitten with her beauty once more. He will not desert me, she thought, and was surprised at her own boldness and confidence.

Beth was moving about, lighting the other lamps so that a mellow glow filled the room. Then she picked up Jacintha's ruined clothes and took them into the bathroom.

"*Like* her?" Beth paused beside Jacintha with a significant leer appearing at the corners of her mouth. "He likes no woman, in the way you most likely mean. He likes a female body, that is all. And Mrs. Anson's seems to please him as well as any around here."

Jacintha felt a sharp little prickle of jealous shock and anxiety.

"It does?" Jacintha did not look at Beth but continued studying herself in the mirror as she picked up a gold and crystal bottle of rose perfume and touched it to her ears and wrists and throat.

"He's been with her more than with anyone else, I think, since she came. Of course, that isn't to say he doesn't sometimes neglect her for weeks or months at a time. Perhaps even years." Beth shrugged. "But that's him. That's the way he is. It's not sour grapes, madam, but I'm glad I'm not the type for him."

Jacintha looked up at her. "You're glad? You mean

to say that you prefer to have neither joy nor pain? You'll do without joy in order to avoid the pain?"

"That's what I mean, madam."

"You must have had more spirit when you were alive or they'd never have burned you for a witch."

"It wasn't anything *I* did, madam. I had the ill luck to be born with one blue eye and one brown eye. And that was what brought about my fate."

"Only that?" demanded Jacintha, incredulous.

"Only that." Beth nodded vigorously, and bent down so that Jacintha could inspect her one brown eye and one blue eye.

"Thank heaven, I didn't live in such a barbarous age."

Beth went into the bathroom. "Didn't you?"

Jacintha watched her go, annoyed by the impertinent remark, then shrugged her shoulders and stood up, still admiring herself.

She had never realized how alluring a dressing gown could be with nothing under it. Of course, even with Martin she had worn her petticoats and camisole. Now, its deeply opened neck showed her breasts, swelling out, the nipples soft and relaxed from the room's warmth. Jacintha posed, bending slightly and gracefully one way and then another. Then, suddenly embarrassed, she straightened, drew the gown together, gave a toss of her head, and went to sit in one of the chairs, looking automatically about for some needlework to occupy her hands.

Of course, there was none.

Beth appeared once more. "What am I going to do?" asked Jacintha.

"About what, madam?"

"About my time. No one packed any books or any Berlin work or anything at all for me to *do*. Can I buy some materials somewhere?"

"Not that I know of, madam."

"You mean the women here don't do needlework or make things?"

"Not that I know of, madam."

"Then what do they do?"

"Whatever they can think of."

"Well, I'm going to get some patterns and some yarn and begin to work on something. I cannot be idle."

Beth was folding garments now, watching her with a look of curiosity and sadness. "You mean to do needlework all through eternity?"

"All through." Jacintha stopped, overtaken once more by that sick, plunging despair: *You mean to do needlework all through eternity?*

"Well, why not?" she demanded. "What else is there to do? You mean, he's provided no diversions for us?"

"He's provided *himself,* madam . . . for some of you, anyway."

"I, as it happens," retorted Jacintha, "intend to have nothing to do with him."

Beth gave her a sly smile. "You mean to say you prefer neither joy nor pain?"

"Don't talk to me like that!" cried Jacintha, and she jumped up in a sudden flash of anger. "Use sarcasm on me and I'll slap your face."

"Yes, madam."

"I mean it! Oh—no, I don't." She sighed. "I'm sorry, Beth. Of course I won't slap you. I'm sorry I was rude. But I'm out of my mind!" She was wringing her hands now. "To be here in this terrible place forever!" Her voice had risen to a hysterical wail. Beth came quickly and put her arms about her, holding her gently and patting her shoulders and back.

"I know, madam, I know. It's a hard thought to get used to. It's better not to think about it. Just go along from day to day . . . as you did before."

Gently, Jacintha disengaged herself and wandered slowly about the room, pausing now and again to touch a fringe on a chair, to examine a red velvet sofa covering, to tinkle the beads hanging on a glass lampshade. "If he doesn't provide for us, then I shall provide for myself. Tomorrow I'm going to go out and get some ferns and flowers, mosses and twigs and set to work myself."

"What sort of work will you do with those materials, madam?"

"Why, I'll make lampshades and little boxes and things of that kind. And I'll start to collect curiosities. This is a fine place for curiosities. I shall begin a collection of pressed flowers, too. And I will set aside a certain time every day to go botanizing and educate myself on the plants of the vicinity. And I will—'' She stopped, covered her face with her hands, and began to cry. ''It was all right to do those things when I was alive. I enjoyed it. But who can do them forever?''

Then her sobs broke beyond restraint. Beth sorrowfully watched her as if she knew that it would do no good to offer comfort. Jacintha stood with her face covered, her shoulders shaking, weeping harder and harder. *To have nothing to do...*

We don't realize, Cherry had said, how greatly we depend on our duties. She had also said: He offers the only hope there is in this crowded, desolate place.

It had sounded incredible at the time, yet now it seemed so clear and obvious.

That is why she was ready to destroy me when I threatened to take her place with him. And that is why I hate her now.

She heard a soft hiss and looked up swiftly.

It was Beth, standing beside the doorway into the hall, holding it slightly ajar. Now she jerked her head. ''She's coming!''

''Who?''

''Mrs. Anson. Quick! You can see her.''

Jacintha hesitated on the edge of haughty refusal, but then she picked up her ruffled skirts and rushed to the door. Of course she wanted to see her. She wanted to see how she looked. And, anyway, what else did she have to do? Idleness, interminable idleness, would produce considerable changes in her, she could see that now.

Jacintha stood beside Beth and peeked out. The hall, as usual, was rather dimly lit, but they could see Cherry hurrying toward them, moving with her familiar, graceful little steps. She was still only a distant figure but, after a few moments, she emerged more clearly and they could see that her gown was drenched, tangled, and torn, her hair undone and hanging in wet coils across her breasts and over her shoulders. Her entire appearance was wild, disheveled, at once rapturous and tormented. She had been, it seemed, entirely possessed. Cherry radiated an aura of enchantment.

Jacintha was outraged.

She heard Beth give a little clucking sound and suddenly became aware of the girl's warm body and the faintly unpleasant smell she had. She turned and gestured her away, ignoring the look of disappointment and pleading on her face. What right had that wretched creature to stand gaping at her mother's shameful appearance?

Cherry came along swiftly. Just as she drew opposite the door and passed beneath one of the gas jets, her face looming unbelievably large, she was wholly absorbed in private thoughts and feelings.

Nevertheless, just as she passed, Jacintha stepped back and shut the door. After a moment she opened it again and this time stepped into the hallway. Cherry was opening her own door and now, as if at a signal, she turned slowly and faced her daughter.

Jacintha gave a start as those dark eyes rested upon her, feeling as if she had caught a culprit and, at the same time, been guilty of a crime. She stepped hastily back and closed the door.

Breathing fast and hard, weak from some inexplicable terror, her heart pounding so that her whole body shook, Jacintha leaned against the wall helplessly. She was convinced that something peculiarly horrible had been about to happen between them and that it would have happened, but for her own swift retreat.

Cherry's face, a white mask with dark, glowing eyes, seemed to brand her mind's eye as if she had gazed too long at the sun.

Beth crept nearer, like a frightened pup. "What did she do, madam? What did she do?"

Jacintha ignored her for a few moments, still fighting for self-control. Then, suddenly enraged at Beth's whining insistence, she flared out, "Don't you know who she is?"

"Who is she, madam?" repeated Beth, trembling now, as if Jacintha had threatened to beat her. "She's Mrs. Anson, madam . . . isn't she?"

"Oh, you're so stupid!" cried Jacintha, disgusted to hear herself speak that way to a servant. She stood with her back to the fireplace and then addressed Beth very clearly. "Mrs. Anson is my mother."

Beth retreated as from a blow. "Oh," she whispered. "How cruel. How *cruel*." She was shaking her head, and her distress was so genuine that Jacintha felt not only pity for her but honest affection as well, and she smiled, trying with gentleness to make up for the way she had spoken earlier.

"Yes, it is cruel, isn't it? I suppose it amuses him greatly."

Beth was silent a moment, thinking over this startling information. Then she lifted her head and looked at Jacintha once more. "Which of you will renounce him? Since even I can see that you love him too, madam."

"*I* will, of course!" retorted Jacintha. "Who else? I have done it already."

Beth shrugged and gestured, palms up. "God give you strength." And suddenly, realizing what she had said, she clapped both hands to her mouth, stared at Jacintha a moment with her eyes popped wide, and then they laughed together at the blunder.

"I think I'll go to bed now," said Jacintha finally. "I'm very tired and perhaps I can sleep."

Beth turned down the bed and went puttering about the room, straightening furniture and picking up odds and ends: a fan Jacintha had played with for a few moments, a hairpin she had dropped. Then she turned out the lamps. Beth left one burning, for Jacintha was still standing before the fire, yawning and stretching, watching the flames, admiring their colors that kept blending and changing, like a liquid opal.

"Good night, now, madam."

"Good night, Beth."

The door closed and the girl was gone. Jacintha sighed. She continued to stand, watching the fire, one hand lightly poised on her hip, leaning with her other arm against the mantelpiece. Idly, her eyes traveled down to her toes and up her bare leg, which emerged in a taut, straight line from the gown's opened front, showing as far as her thigh. The light turned her flesh a melting rosy tone that she could not help admiring, and then, impulsively, she slid free of the gown and flung it onto a chair, kicked off her slippers, and stood naked before the fire, luxuriously enjoying the heat on her skin.

How good it feels. How wicked I am standing here like this. Jacintha was surprised to find herself indifferent to the discovery.

The fire seemed to eat into her skin, nibbling at her flesh, rousing urgent sensual and voluptuous longings. All this beauty, she reflected dreamily. Jacintha was filled with yearning to have herself desired, to watch a man's responses as he gloated over her, to see his mounting excitement and, finally, to abandon herself to his mastery.

It hasn't taken long for me to grow accustomed to this place.

Slowly she turned, very slowly, for she wanted to surprise her own image in the mirror. Across the room, pretending by casting her eyes this way and that, she did not quite know where she would encounter herself. And, with that same self-absorbed, dreamy expression, her body languidly turning, she encountered him, instead.

He stood a few feet away, at the top of the trapdoor stairs, where Grant had appeared the night before.

He had one foot planted on the carpet, the other on

the stairs, and he leaned forward so that one arm rested across his leg. He was fully clothed, wearing informal evening dress, and smiling broadly.

She gave a shriek of alarm and stumbled backward.

Recovering herself, she rushed to get her dressing gown. But as she reached for it he moved swiftly, snatching it from the tips of her fingers and kicking the trapdoor shut.

"What do you need it for?"

"I'm naked! Oh, please give it to me! *Please!*"

Jacintha watched in stunned disbelief as he ripped the garment apart, tossing the halves at her, still laughing.

He began to wander about the room, his hands in his pockets, as if he had come on a tour of inspection.

Jacintha stood there holding the pieces in her hands. Her embarrassment was intensified because he was fully clothed.

He prowled about, his expression amused but watchful, as if anything found wrong or out of place might annoy him. He picked up one of her embroidered pincushions, examined it for a moment, and tossed it down. He looked at some of her bottles and boxes full of handkerchiefs and jewelry. He opened a drawer or two and closed them again with the toe of his shining black leather shoe. Finally he turned.

"Is everything to your satisfaction?"

"Oh, yes," said Jacintha, holding the torn wrapper before her and feeling like a fool. With all the beautiful clothes she had, all the things she would have liked him to see her in, she was standing there holding two shredded muslin rags.

Apparently he found it as ridiculous as she, for now he crossed the room, snatched them away from her, tossed them into a heap, and said, "Stop that nonsense. You've got a beautiful body and you know it. You're longing to have me look at you, so stop pretending. Where did this modesty come from?"

He was right, of course. She did want him to look at her. And yet, she felt so helpless and absurd. "But I can't look dignified!" she protested. "I—I feel awkward."

"You look," he said slowly, "as white and succulent as the flesh of an apple."

"Oh..." breathed Jacintha. "I do?" Her hands dropped to her sides.

Then she remembered what had happened this afternoon. It was incredible she could have forgotten for even a moment. Of course, he had appeared in his usual sudden, startling fashion and caught her off guard. Now she had returned to her senses and would treat him as he deserved, with a full measure of hauteur, intimidating to any male upon whom she had ever turned its powerful beam. She would wilt his confidence, shrivel his despotic assurance.

Preparing to impale him with a look of disdain, she lifted her brows, faced him directly, and felt herself begin to melt inside.

For this man seemed to her a species of idol, something too beautiful and mysterious for her comprehension. How dare she judge him? This was his world, not hers.

There he stood, calm and self-contained. And all at
once she was swept with a memory so violent its force
seemed great enough to crush her.

"Thank you," she said humbly, "for the compli-
ment."

"It's quite true," he replied.

The longer he looked, the less embarrassed she felt.
Since he would not permit her to be shyly modest, there
was no reason to pretend that she was. Was this not, after
all, exactly what she had been wishing for only moments
before he had appeared?

She even had a sense that she was being permitted to
satisfy a wish she had cherished, to be naked and stared at
by a man. Neither her husband nor Brian had thought it
proper to show undue interest in her naked body, though
Brian, being her lover, had taken a greater and franker
interest than her husband. With them both she had always
assumed a role of exaggerated shyness.

How delightful it was finally to have had her beauty
discovered. It seemed to her that by his admiration and
interest, he had made her truly beautiful for the first time.
What meaning had her loveliness had before, only covertly
enjoyed and usually half ignored?

Very slowly, in a movement as fluid as oil poured
from a jar, she raised up on her toes, drew her ribs high so
that her waist narrowed to its smallest circle, lifted her
breasts and raised her arms above her head, sweeping her
long black hair upward.

Quickly then, smiling at him with her head tipped

slightly forward, she divided her hair into two sections and tied a knot. The gesture was simple, almost innocent, yet she was aware of its provocative nature.

He did not move, continuing to watch her. Jacintha felt a sharp, painful twist inside. What was wrong? Why was she not exciting him? And then the humiliating reason struck her. Of course. He was satiated, replete from his afternoon with Cherry. Here she was, confronting him, wanting him to desire her, when the mere notion of a woman was probably tiresome to him.

And yet, they had said he was insatiable.

Then what is he doing? Why is he here? Has he come to humiliate and torment me?

Something of her bewilderment and despair must have shown in her face, for just as she had begun to despise herself for standing there with that ridiculous smile of invitation, he came to her rescue.

"Yes," he said softly, nodding his head. "You are beautiful." He leaned back against a great marble-topped chest, slid his hands into his pockets, crossed his feet, and smiled. "You're as beautiful as any woman I've ever seen."

"What a thing to say!"

"You would have preferred that I said you were *more* beautiful?" he asked.

"I would have preferred," retorted Jacintha, "that you did not make any comparison at all. No woman wants to think a man is running his eye over his private collection while he is with her."

"It's very strange," he said and slowly shook his head.

"What is very strange?"

"You women are all alike—no matter what era you were born in. Your one truly insatiable appetite is for compliments. You call it chivalry in one age, gallantry in another."

"You seem to overlook the fact," she said, "that women are born with a handicap. There is something naturally ridiculous about us and our entire predicament. If we did not protect ourselves by disguising our own absurdity beneath many veils of romantic mist, men would treat us much worse even than they do."

He laughed softly. "You're clever," he said. "Who taught you all this? Your mother died too young, though she would have been an excellent teacher."

"Don't mention my mother!" cried Jacintha, and seemed to hear the cry still in the air, like the sound of tearing silk, long after the words left her mouth.

She leaped up and ran to stand before him, so furiously angry that she had lost all fear of him. He had not moved but continued to stand with his hands in his pockets, looking at her with an indifference that was quite majestic.

"*You—!*" she began, in a frenzy of rage and hatred.

He seized her wrists with one hand and gave a quick twist that sent her spinning. She regained her footing, then whirled and rushed at him again. He was walking toward her now, advancing slowly, and she stopped still, then turned to run away, when she heard his voice: "Come here!"

She stood where she was, trembling and waiting, and when his hand took hold of her shoulder she began to quiver uncontrollably. As he turned her to face him, she raised her hands as if to ward off a blow.

A look of disgust crossed his face and he shook his head. "No," he said. "Don't do that. What have I ever done to make you think I'd hurt you?"

Her hands dropped and she was looking at him with wondering despair.

"I don't know," she replied weakly. "I'm afraid of you. I think that you despise me. I think you came here to mock me." She lifted her face higher and looked up at him now with perfect open honesty. "Why *did* you come tonight?"

"I wanted to see you."

"No," she said sadly. "You came to remind me of what happened last night between us and of what happened this afternoon between you and my mother."

He stood looking at her, his eyes slightly narrowed as if he were concentrating closely, not upon her face or body, but rather on her essence as a woman. "You know," he said at last, "your mother was no older than you when she died. But she has much more sense about men."

"Ohhh—" Jacintha gave a lonely, protesting little wail. She turned, covering her face with her hands, and dropped slowly to the floor at his feet.

He cares nothing about me. She knows how to please him better than I do. What does she do? What does she know? I defeat myself every moment. And yet, I do know better. It must be something in him that makes me do the wrong things.

She heard a soft sound and looked up. He was walking away from her.

"Are you going?"

He turned when she spoke and paused, looking back. "Yes. I'm going."

There was nothing of the desire she had seen on his face last night. He was looking at her as if she were a pitiful child. How could she have imagined that only a few hours after their lovemaking he could look at her as if it had never happened or as if he, at least, had forgotten?

For that is the thing. A woman can never believe that once a man leaves her body he can be entirely free of her—that he can regain his self-possession as easily as he had lost it. He can consider her or not, as he chooses, without reference to their intimacy. There is no imprisonment, unless he seeks it, for himself.

"Are you crying?" He seemed honestly puzzled.

She gave a soft, bitter little laugh. "I love you—that's all it is. I want you, one way or another, all the time."

After a momentary shock at hearing herself, there came a surprised feeling that she had abandoned the battlefield to a rival general. She was exquisitely glad that she need never deceive either of them again.

He did not move, but there was a look on his face now

that seemed close to compassion—certainly there was sympathy. Yet there was not, as she had hoped, a return of that sudden lust that had transformed him, and her, the night before.

"You want a great deal," he said slowly, "for a woman so recently a lady."

"I want more from you than I could ever have guessed."

She kept waiting, expecting him to do something. He only stood and continued looking at her, and he seemed to her incomparably brilliant, spectacular, and remote. "There may be times," he said finally, "when you will regret what has happened to you."

"What is it that I am going to regret?"

"Many things, I suppose. Brian, for one. Me. You won't be able to help yourself, and I can't help you, either."

"If you wanted to . . ."

He shook his head. "I don't want to."

"And you never will?"

"I never will."

Jacintha looked down again. Her eyes had begun to ache, as if the terrible intensity of her desire had concentrated there. She yearned for him with a tormenting ardor that she felt would be unendurable if it were not appeased. But she was helpless, dependent upon him, while he was entirely detached from her. She would never have the comfortable, necessary feminine conviction of holding and possessing him.

He would remain as he was, inaccessible, appearing

and disappearing according to his own need, without reference to her; while she must somehow learn to endure the taunting loneliness of waiting, of patience, of brief joy and endless anxiety.

This, she supposed, was what she would regret.

Or had she been, as he had said, in love with him for a long while and eager to reach her destination?

"No," she agreed. "I know you won't. And will you never love me, either, even if I do everything right?"

"You can't do everything right, since I have no definition of what is wrong. But if you know the answer, why did you ask?"

"I suppose I asked because I was hoping . . . "

"You were hoping that you would be the one exception?"

She lifted her head quickly, her face lively and alert, almost flirtatious, to conceal, if possible, her embarrassment and profound, hopeless disappointment. "And I'm not."

"Of course not. I told you yesterday, when you asked me. I don't fall in love. It's not one of the things that happens to me. You know, there is always something which a given woman lacks. But I have never yet met one who had a deficiency of vanity." His expression had changed again, and some slight hint of mockery had returned.

"I know," agreed Jacintha apologetically. "It was foolish of me to ask. And yet, it was a natural thing to do, wasn't it?"

He nodded. "Perfectly natural for you to want me to

love you. And perfectly natural for me not to do so. Good night.''

"You're not going!''

He crossed the room and gave a sharp stamp of his foot. The trapdoor flew open and there was Grant, disgusting and offensive as always, with his uncanny grin. Jacintha shrieked and bent over, covering herself with her hands. "Get on down there!'' he said sharply. Grant disappeared from view.

Jacintha leaped up and ran to him. Cool moisture came from the stairwell and her flesh crept with the cold. "Take me with you!''

He descended two or three steps and regarded her as she stood there, looking desolate, and yet so beautiful in her eagerness and honest self-betrayal. "I don't think so,'' he murmured, still smiling.

Hopeful, because he had not absolutely refused, Jacintha reached out and touched his arms, her face almost level with his now; she was shivering in the wet cold.

Grant had left a lantern on the top step, and it threw strange, sharp shadows that lit their faces eerily. "Please, please,'' she whispered. "Please.''

His mouth was very near and her eyes closed. Her lips parted and waited, endlessly it seemed, until, at last, she felt the slow, warm pressure of his mouth. She sighed and her arms passed swiftly and eagerly about his shoulders, her breasts crushing the stiff white front of his shirt. The memory of last night had tormented her throughout the day, in spite of everything she had attempted to banish it, yet now that it was happening once more it was infinitely more exciting and rewarding, more fulfilling to the intolerable emptiness she had begun to feel.

Her passion sprang eagerly, like an animal rushing to greet its master, then crouching for a moment, obediently waiting for his sign. He released her and moved away, while she regarded him with startled eyes and increasing despair. He went down another step.

"No!" she cried "*I'm* coming!"

She descended, her face again level with his. She stared into his eyes, pleading and scared, for she knew now that he did not intend to let her accompany him. He was smiling at her again.

"Run along," he said, "before you take a chill."

She continued to stare at him, determined to prevent his departure for as long as possible. Even if there was nothing more he would give her, she wanted his presence—only to look at him was a greater pleasure than any she had had with another man. But then his face changed once more, and she knew that he was through playing with her. She must obey. She turned and slowly walked back up and stood at the top of the stairs, looking wistfully down. His face turned up to her, the lantern casting bold shadows on it. She gazed at him with longing admiration. She was not even angry. She gave another sigh, this one heavy and hopeless.

He had succeeded, again, in dominating her. But, whereas the night before, he had accomplished this through tenderness and, later, physical power, tonight there had been nothing more definable than his clear and absolute self-possession. He had no understanding of what it was to crave something inaccessible, to yearn, to lie in torment and anguish, waiting, lonely, frightened, angry, hating and loving at once. These things belonged to another breed, and in them he found nothing that was tragic or that obligated him.

"When will I see you again?" she asked finally.

"I don't know."

She suddenly foresaw the night and the next day and perhaps a thousand more days or even years. She grew wildly frantic. "But what will I do while I wait for you?" she implored. "What is there for me to do?"

He shrugged.

"I asked my maid today and she says you don't even have embroidery needles here!"

He smiled. "She's right. I don't have embroidery needles."

"You don't have yarn or glue or paints or any of the things I must have to keep myself busy."

"Is that how you kept yourself busy?" he inquired, as if vaguely admiring this manner of occupation.

"Of course!" she cried. The thought occurred to her that if she could engage him in a quarrel, she could keep him with her a little longer. Perhaps he would take her with him after all. "I was always busy. I was never idle. But no one packed my books or my paints or my Berlin work. I have nothing to do! You have provided nothing for our diversion."

He listened, and his eyebrows flickered slightly. "On the other hand," he said, in an eminently reasonable tone, "how could I provide for your diversion? Each generation of rich women has a different way of wasting time. The poor spend their lives having babies and trying to make ends meet. The poor women who are pretty enough to get in here have an opportunity to dress and live like the rich. They think it's Heaven, for a century or two. No, Jacintha. I have not provided for your diversion. The problem here is one of too much leisure, and each of us must solve it in his own way. You will have to find what means you can of passing eternity. You can regard it, if you like—and I think it will be helpful if you do—as a challenge, a problem in imagination and resourcefulness. I don't mean to sound pessimistic, but I've been here a long while and from my own experiences and what I've heard of others', I don't think it is possible to succeed in that task. Things are quite pleasant here, as I'm sure you will agree—" He gestured to indicate the handsome, luxuriously furnished room. "And yet, everyone is dissatisfied, myself included. I'm afraid the truth is that any heaven would become hell if it lasted too long. Good night."

He descended rapidly, reaching up with one swift movement of his arm and shutting the trapdoor with a crash. At the last instant, as she moved forward, crying out, a flashing half-smile appeared on his somber, dark face so unexpectedly, shone brilliantly for such a brief moment, that now, with the door fast shut and its outline lost once more in the carpet's intricate pattern, she continued to see the gleaming black eyes, the trace of white teeth beneath his scarcely parted lips, the look of tantalizing challenge.

Then, as the image slowly faded, she thought perhaps he had not been there at all.

Yet he had. For his kiss had brought all her desire for him into focus. And now he was gone, leaving her full of unease and discontent.

The fire burned down. The room grew chilly and she realized that she was cold, even shivering. She turned out the lamp and crept into bed where she lay with her teeth chattering, stretched out straight and flat, staring into the black room, eager and alert, still convinced that he would return to her. She waited, intently listening. She scarcely gave any thought to what he had told her at the last, or to what kind of predicament she was in . . . only listening, her muscles tight and ready to leap. The time passed slowly and she continued waiting, refusing to believe that he would not return. Suddenly there was a sharp crack, and she gave a violent, shuddering start.

"Yes!" she cried, and sat up straight. "Who is it? Who's there?"

She waited, her heart pounding, not knowing whether he had reentered the room. At last, she got out of bed and lit a lamp. The room was empty.

I was falling asleep, she decided. It was the fireplace cooling off that made that sound.

She turned out the light and went back to bed,

continuing to listen until, slowly, against her will and almost without her knowledge, her muscles unknotted, relaxed, and she fell asleep.

When she awoke, Beth was bustling about the room, the fire was going, and the draperies were drawn back, letting in the brilliant morning sunshine. As she opened her eyes, Beth cried out cheerfully: "Good morning, madam!"

Jacintha sighed. She glanced at the clock; it was only nine. She had not slept very long and she was tired. But worse than that, she felt overwhelmed by a morbid, hopeless gloom.

"Good morning, Beth. Have you been here long?"

"An hour or so, madam, I should say. I've sent for your breakfast. It will give you something to do, so I thought you might like to have it. You can sit by this window and look out. It's *such* a fine day!"

"It seems always to be *such* a fine day in this place. Isn't it ever dreary? Where's my wrapper? Oh—" she said, as she remembered.

Beth apparently had seen it already, for a roguish grin spread over her face as she picked up the two shredded rags and held them before Jacintha: "You had a visitor, I see."

"Stop that!" cried Jacintha, and clapped her hands together. "You're the most impertinent creature I've ever had for a servant. Get my wrapper."

"Yes, madam. I'm sorry, madam. I thought we'd have a laugh together."

"I can't imagine what there is to laugh at," muttered Jacintha. Beth brought her another dressing gown. Her slippers were there, just beside her bed, and she stood up, throwing back her head and shaking out her long black hair, running her fingers through it.

"Only that it's exactly like him, madam, to do a thing of that kind. And though I'm sure you were warned against him many times, as we all were, you let him dupe you all the same. But I'm sorry if the mention of it offends you, madam." She hurried across the room and began to clear the little tulipwood desk that stood between the two big windows.

Jacintha watched her moodily, sorry for her, angry that she would dare be on such familiar terms with her, something she had never before permitted in a servant—but glad, too, for the mere fact of her presence. Now there was a rap at the door and Beth went to get the tray which one of the lackeys delivered. On it was Jacintha's breakfast and, as Beth bore it swiftly to the desk, she could smell the buckwheat cakes and sausages and coffee. Beth arranged the pretty hand-painted dishes, placing each one as if it gave her pleasure, then stepped back with a little gesture for Jacintha to take her place.

Jacintha sat down humbly. "Thank you. I won't—I won't snap at you again, Beth."

"Oh, I don't mind, madam. I know your nerves must be strung like a harp. He *is* a hard one, isn't he?"

Jacintha, spreading the napkin in her lap and removing the silver covers from the dishes, nodded her head.

"He is," she agreed with a sigh. "He is. But they never mentioned the way he looks. In fact, they pretended he was ugly."

"Of course! If women knew what charms he has, what use would they have for other men? He makes all other men look ugly and seem like dullards, doesn't he?"

Jacintha nodded, picking indifferently at her plate. "He does, that's true. But he's capricious and he's cruel. He taunts and mocks and ridicules, and I can't and won't endure that kind of treatment." The words sounded to her like the delayed echo of something spoken long ago in a hollow room.

"Still, madam," said Beth, as she turned to pull the blankets and sheets off the bed and make it up fresh, "what else is there for you to do?"

At that, Jacintha put down her fork and sat staring out the window, across the meadows with their whirling steam and rushing torrents of hot water, and over the low, pine-covered hills to the dim mountains beyond. A kind of languid stupor seemed to invade her; finally she sighed.

"Then, resolutely, she got up. "I'll find something to do!" she announced. "I'll begin by taking a bath."

She made as much of the bath as she could, lingering in it until she was all but immobilized by the heat. Then she dawdled over getting dressed, searching through her closet, discussing this gown and that one with Beth. Finally they selected one made of bright green wool with black stripes running up and down the bodice and cross-wise over the gathered skirt. Beth took some time to put up her hair. Then there was the business of selecting gloves, hat, jewelry, and parasol.

But the closer she came to being dressed, the slower her movements got and the more her hands and, it seemed, her whole insides, began to tremble with apprehension. She grew heavy in every muscle, as if her arms and legs dragged great weights: Why should she go out? What was there to do?

She faced herself in the mirror, staring with hostile indifference as though at an unwelcome stranger. She looked enchantingly beautiful, and she despised the sight of herself. She wore a hat, black kid gloves, carried a parasol and handbag in her right hand, and a fan in her left. Her face, white and oddly tragic, gazed back at her. She stood in this way for several moments while Beth hovered about, looking vaguely frightened and full of concern.

She fell to thinking of him with resentment and something she thought might be hatred. But his beauty, and the vivid memories of what he had given her, changed in an instant from anger to longing, from regret to gratitude.

"Madam—" Beth whispered at last, extending her hand tentatively— "Are you ready?"

Jacintha sighed and nodded. "Yes. Shall we go now?"

Slowly she walked to the door and Beth opened it. She went through the doorway, took two steps, and then turned and looked toward Cherry's door.

She had been trying all night to keep Cherry out of her thoughts. They loved the same man and hated each other. There was no place in their lives for companionship or even tolerance. They were never to meet again—never to speak to each other.

She felt that old desolation, that emptiness, that hopeless longing for her mother's voice, her smile and comforting arms, the warmth of her love and devotion denied her since childhood.

It was as if she had taken the memories of her mother into her own body, shrouded, concealed, and cherished them. These feelings had been a part of herself; a pain, most terrible and intense, that must not be touched.

Must I do all that again?

I can't.

Shaking her head, Jacintha turned and walked back into her room. She sat beside the window once more, her black-gloved hands shielding her face as she rested her elbows on the desktop.

"I'm not going out," she said to Beth. "I can't."

She felt a peculiar stranger inside herself. She retired into dazed seclusion, waiting until she could face the pain, permit it to enter her and reestablish itself. She could not allow it to rush in all at once. The pain was a horrible specter, which must move into her house little by little, slowly making room for itself, pushing other feelings out of the way until it had the space it needed. At that moment it might grow obstreperous and destroy the entire fabric of her being. That had almost happened at the time of her mother's death. And yet, just when it threatened to break down the boundaries of her being, she had forced it to wait, to let her grow a bit larger in order to contain it. And the pain had lived within her ever since.

Then she and Cherry had met here. She had thought she was rid of her companion forever.

But now it was back, demanding admission. She sat pretending to be unaware of it battering away at her.

We were so entirely happy. It almost seemed we had made up for all the years after she died. The instant we found each other here I experienced that mystical happiness, that blend of tenderness and mercy and compassion, arising out of something deeper in us than love for a man.

As she sat there, her head in her hands, Jacintha sank into a kind of stupor, drifting backward through the centuries, the millennia that had produced all women. That continuity of blood seemed the only true, eternal value, which she now perceived with perfect clarity, significant only as it had passed from Cherry to herself.

I must go and talk to her.

Jacintha was devoted to her relationship with Cherry and to all the women whose bodies had given them life. She felt a tie stronger than any she had formed before, an existence no relationship with a man had ever touched. Here was loyalty. Here was her link with all humanity. Her passion for him could no longer be permitted to interfere with the deep oceanic love that flowed between Cherry and herself.

If only she were not a beautiful woman my own age . . .

I wish she were beyond her youth and loveliness; of course, that would make it simple. And I would be gentle with her and perfectly in command because of my own youth and beauty.

I am selfish. I deserve to be unhappy!

We have met each other honestly here, each of us at the height of beauty and energy and desirability. He wants to destroy our love, to entertain himself with his brief mischief. But we must be more clever than he. We must not permit him to do it.

Jacintha leaped to her feet and whirled about, to face Cherry coming through the doorway as Beth backed out, bowing her head and closing the door behind her.

The two women confronted each other.

Cherry looked calm, almost serene, and there was a slight smile on her lips, one with no mockery or cruelty in it, only tenderness and love. Jacintha's body was tense, her eyes big and staring. With a little moan, she ran forward and Cherry rushed to meet her. They flung their arms about each other. Jacintha was crying and Cherry stroked her back and patted her.

After a few minutes Jacintha dried her eyes and blew her nose.

"We won't let him do it, will we?" asked Cherry softly.

Jacintha shook her head vigorously.

"No, we won't!"

But then Cherry said, "Still, I've known him longer than you, Jacintha, and I think I can say with reasonable authority that in a sense he is worse than we were told. Oh, not in any obvious way. He is, after all, tremendously attractive and desirable and exciting. But we are accustomed to one way of life—and he to another. Don't you see?"

"I'm . . . not sure," admitted Jacintha.

Cherry sat in one of the crimson velvet chairs, crossing her delicate ankles, holding the handle of her parasol in one gloved hand, the other resting lightly in her lap. Her small bonnet had a veil that tied across her face and cast tiny dots of shadow on it. She looked delightfully young and fresh. Once more, now that they were together, Jacintha found it impossible to keep in mind that this vivacious, merry young woman was her mother.

"While it is happening," said Cherry, speaking in her soft, gentle tone, "it is impossible to feel more than enormous gratitude. After all, he is a brilliant lover. But later, doubt and dissatisfaction set in. He leaves one nothing but anticipation of the next time. In that way, he robs us of the future, and also of the past. What is left to us is but a tenuous memory, only enough to taunt, but not enough to satisfy."

She tilted her head to one side as she regarded her daughter, who looked perplexed and unhappy. "There is neither punishment nor reward. And so, it is useless and worse than useless. It depresses and frightens us. And yet—" She gestured despairingly with her free hand— "We have nothing else. He is absolute master."

"We have each other!"

Cherry smiled. "We have." She nodded slightly. "We have each other, of course. You know that I love you, Jacintha. I know that you love me. We would not, either of us, willingly hurt the other. But we have hated each other. And I'm afraid we shall again."

"No!" cried Jacintha. "We won't! If you want him—have him. I don't . . ." She waved her hands excitedly, almost as if his image had appeared before her eyes and she was trying to brush it away. "I don't want anything more to do with him! I've seen him clearly. I know what he is now. I give him to you." Unaware of what she was doing, Jacintha mimed gathering a gift into her two hands, then leaned forward with a sweeping bow, and presented it to Cherry.

Cherry threw back her head and laughed joyously. "Oh, Jacintha! Jacintha, darling!"

Jacintha, shocked and offended, straightened and stared down at her. "I beg your pardon?"

"You're so sweet, darling. And so innocent."

Jacintha did not like being treated in this fashion, as if she were a naïve and rather dull-witted child. What right had Cherry to mock her intense desire to please, her renunciation of future pleasure with him? Why should she not be humbly grateful that her daughter was willing to give up so much for her? How dare she laugh?

"Don't, sweetheart," said Cherry teasingly, and pursed her full, pink lips. "Don't look so cross with me. I think you're charming and touching and adorable. But *how* can you give him up? Tell me, while we were alive, what was the source of most of our joy and much of our hope?"

"Why—I suppose—"

"That's not a difficult riddle," said Cherry briskly. "You know what it was as well as I. It was physical love. Nothing else. Oh, we pretend that it was a great many other things. And if I had lived, I suppose I would have been hypocritical enough to tell you that it was many other things, too. Neither of us would have been fooled, of course. Now what have you to say?"

Jacintha stood for several moments, staring at Cherry in turbulent confusion—hurt and dismayed.

"I don't believe you!"

Politely and coolly, Cherry lifted her brows. "What is it, then, we value more?"

Jacintha felt that in some profound and disturbing way, she had been tricked and then cheated. All her life she had believed in her mother as a virtuous and noble lady, a paragon of womanhood.

And these were the things she believed in?

Well then, it was her duty to defeat that image and set herself in its place.

I will save us.

The thought that she would rescue them both gave

her a sense of conviction and strength—a capacity for self-abnegation she had never known she possessed.

"There is so much more," Jacintha said solemnly. "What you have mentioned," she said slowly, speaking with careful disdain, "is not the greatest, but the *least* of the glories of humanity."

She spoke so fervently that she had convinced herself and thus forgotten not only the time she had spent with him but his challenging and monumental beauty, as well.

Cherry lifted one eyebrow, slowly twirling her ruffled parasol as she balanced its tip against the floor. "Indeed?" she asked softly. She looked amused but tolerant, too.

"There are so *many* noble things in life. . . ." Jacintha flung out both arms in a furious gesture and walked to the window. The blood seemed to be rushing through her body in a torrent, and she could feel herself begin to perspire with anxiety. She whirled about. "There are so many things!" she cried. "To begin with, there is a mother's love for her children."

"Yes," agreed Cherry, her head high and alert, her tone gently humorous. "But your children are not here."

"But yours is!" cried Jacintha and then stopped, feeling that in some way she had betrayed herself.

Something terrible had happened.

She had said the wrong thing.

What was it?

She had meant so well, had felt herself to be exalted and ennobled, yet without warning, there had been some hideous self-betrayal.

Jacintha waited for what Cherry would say now, expecting that she would take this opportunity to destroy her.

But Cherry did nothing of the kind. Lifting her brows and glancing away, she merely said lightly, "Ah, so you are. And, since you are, I suppose I should be the one to . . ."

"You should not be!" broke in Jacintha, for she could not hear her implication put into words. "There are many other things. There is honor and justice, loyalty, consideration and generosity, self-respect, and—"

She would have rushed on, but Cherry interrupted gently, still with that urbane little smile: "And all the virtues in the world cannot make you forget the passage of time, as we both know he can do."

Jacintha turned away. She had had an almost religious sense of virtue, a determination to martyr herself in this cause between them and come out once and for all as the nobler of the two.

How could she ever have guessed that she would harbor any such ambitions against her mother? She was ashamed of herself, as intensely as she had been determined to shame Cherry only a few moments earlier.

Now Cherry spoke again. She still sounded entirely in command of herself—calm, light, and sweet. Apparently this scene was not of the same cataclysmic nature to her that it was to Jacintha.

"There is no value here in being good, don't you see?

No one respects it, no one pretends to practice it. We are all in the same desperate situation and must fight our battle with time any way we can. Sensual love is the only thing that can eternally give us pleasure. For it is new each time it happens.''

Jacintha listened meekly, knowing that everything Cherry had said was true. She would be, as he had told her, dissatisfied by many things, but her feeling for him, involving her being to its last cell, was of such a nature that she believed it would last forever, even if she should never see him again.

"Come, now," Cherry said. "Let's not be dishonest with each other. You would not be here if you had not been a courageous woman."

Jacintha shook her head.

"Of course," said Cherry briskly. "You had courage enough to love a man and act on your love. It takes less courage to remain faithful, after all. I don't expect you to give him up for my sake. If you try, you won't succeed at anything but learning to hate me. Perhaps, together, we can outwit him."

Jacintha looked up. *"How?"* she asked in an eager whisper. She crossed over to Cherry and took her hand.

"He no doubt thinks that he has separated us. He probably laughs to himself every time he thinks of us hating each other—meeting after so many years apart and hating each other because of him." Cherry was talking in a quick, crisp manner now, like a general ordering his troops about the field, confident and self-assured.

"He has been outwitted before, you know—but only by guile, never by force."

"How can we be more clever? Is it even possible?"

Cherry released her hand and began to pace around the room. "I'm not sure. The best we can hope for, probably, is to remain together when he expects us to hate the sight of each other. There's no way of predicting him. He appears when and where you least expect him, and disappoints you if you're waiting for him. We shall not wait, or mope, or quarrel with each other, but keep very busy with a great number of things. We shall botanize and shop and get some paints from the Indians. We will get a harp, too—there are all kinds of musical instruments around here, since they are among the things *he* likes— and we will play and sing duets. We will be very busy, at all times."

"Yes, we will!" cried Jacintha eagerly. "We will keep ourselves so occupied that he will be amazed. Let's go out this very minute. We'll begin to do other things and find new interests. Let's not lose a moment!"

They rushed to the mirror and peered into it, lifting their arms in unison to adjust their hats, pulling down their tight bodices so that they fitted without a crease. Taking each other's hand, they skipped from the room in a flurry of laughter and rustling petticoats.

They sped down the corridor and out the side door by which they had left yesterday afternoon. Picking up their skirts, their gowns bright and colorful against the grass—

Jacintha's green with black stripes, Cherry's black-and-red-checkered wool with scrolls of black braid and terraces of black fringe—they ran on and on across the meadow, glancing at each other now and again and bursting into fresh laughter, and they rounded the corner of the building where the line of coaches and horses waited. They climbed up immediately.

"Go anywhere!" cried Cherry. "Hurry!"

She and Jacintha looked at each other delightedly. The driver snapped his whip and the horses leaped forward. They sped along, past the steaming open vents in the earth, across the flower-laden meadows, down narrow forest lanes. They saw motionless buffalo in the distance and passed startled deer that gazed at them for one instant, then disappeared with miraculous speed. Half-naked Indians went galloping by on their ponies. Cherry and Jacintha bounced up and down in the coach, laughing gleefully, pointing to the marvels of the place as if they were seeing them for the first time.

But a practical thought had occurred to Jacintha and, try as she would, she could not banish it. She must know the answer. She put off asking time and again, but at last she could delay no longer. She turned to Cherry, whose face looked radiant and fresh, her skin pure and smooth in the sunlight, everything about her so felicitous. She was almost heartbreakingly lovely and vital.

"What if he tries to make love to one of us again?" called Jacintha, for they were going so fast, the horses' hooves clattering so loud, the crack of the whip sounding again and again, the wheels banging over the rocky path, that she had to raise her voice.

"Why think about that now?" countered Cherry, as if the question genuinely surprised her.

Jacintha realized that Cherry was much better than she at postponing painful thoughts. Cherry's eyes swept Jacintha's face, and she smiled.

"But Cherry, we have to decide!" Jacintha insisted. "If we don't, then we're no better off than we were before."

"We're no better off anyway," replied Cherry, "if you must know the truth."

"Well!" Jacintha felt as if she had been kicked in the stomach. "Then what were all our plans for?"

"Darling, please," crooned Cherry, and clasped her daughter's hand. "No one expects actually to carry out every plan he makes, don't you know that? We made them as much for the sake of making them as for any other reason. They brought us together when we were on the edge of something disastrous. That, in itself, justifies them, doesn't it? We will carry them out as well as possible, of course. But things are no more certain here than anywhere else."

"You mean, you'll change your course, depending on what happens?"

"Why, *certainly*, darling."

"Well," said Jacintha again, and sank back deep in the seat. "If he tries to make love to you . . . you intend to—"

"I intend . . . Oh, Jacintha. Please. Let's both intend nothing more than goodwill toward each other. With that as a beginning, we must improvise as we go along."

"Cherry," Jacintha said sadly. "Cherry, I'm afraid you're immoral."

Unable to contain herself, Cherry threw back her head and gave a laugh of such surprised delight and exuberance that Jacintha stared at her. "You think I'm immoral! You honestly do, darling, don't you?" She seemed not only amused but pleased, as if Jacintha had said something flattering as well as clever.

But to Jacintha it was beginning to seem that with each passing moment she grew older and Cherry younger. She felt herself growing more prudish, more prim, and narrowly critical. What was happening to her?

Her earlier determination to sacrifice herself for the sake of their mother-daughter relationship seemed considerably less grand in design to her now. In fact, it embodied more cowardice than generosity.

I wonder if I'm beginning to look any different?

Jacintha quickly opened her black velvet drawstring bag and took out her mirror. As she lifted it toward her face she had a premonition that she would find herself grotesquely altered. She expected now to confront a thin-lipped woman with her mouth drawn into a straight line and all the luminosity in her brown eyes, her greatest beauty, turned dim and dull. Her skin would no longer be white and clear with the fresh sheen of youth.

With a guilty little start, she glanced sideways at

Cherry, who was still looking gay and pleased, her head now tipped to one side as she regarded Jacintha with faint, amused curiosity.

"You look lovely," she said. "Were you doubtful?"

Jacintha nodded, embarrassed. "A little."

"I know. So was I, for a time. He loves to do that. Tear a woman's vanity to shreds."

And that was what he had done. He had sent for her the night of her arrival, had behaved toward her with that marvelous tenderness and passion. Then, he had promptly abandoned her to go off with Cherry, appearing next to torment her with his beauty and presence while giving her no satisfaction. Of course she had begun to feel ugly!

Jacintha sighed. "If only he were different. Why is he like this?"

"He probably wonders why we are the way we are. Except that, of course, he doesn't care."

A sudden noise caused them to face each other with a look of great surprise and alarm. They twisted about in their seats to see a swarm of mounted Indians round a corner and come galloping straight at them.

"Faster!" screamed Cherry. "Faster! We're being overtaken!"

The Indians, unlike those who had passed earlier, were pursuing them. Feathers flying, covered with bright paint and sending forth a continuous quavering howl which rose and fell, they rode at frenzied speed, and it seemed certain that in another moment they would go sweeping over them, trample them into the mud, and swarm on their way, still howling.

The two women, kneeling on the seat facing backward, clung together and stared in fascinated horror at their fast-approaching pursuers. Their teeth were chattering and they shook from head to foot.

"We'll be scalped!" screamed Jacintha.

"They have the most horrible tortures!"

"Will they rape us?"

"That's the *best* we can hope for!"

The horsemen were fifty yards behind and gaining. Their hoofbeats sounded like continuous thunder. They were all grinning, a sight unbelievably horrifying for the grins appeared to have been pasted across skulls painted black and white and green, red, and yellow. They held their bows ready to shoot and swung tomahawks about their heads.

Suddenly one Indian broke free with such a burst of speed that he seemed literally to fly toward them.

There was a shout, and their coach came to a jolting stop which threw them out of their seats. As the carriage stopped they covered their heads.

He laughed.

They looked up to see him astride his black stallion. He wore a loincloth, beaded moccasins, and a vast feathered headdress. He lacked only the paint to be in full Indian war regalia. Their expressions quickly shifted from astonishment and fear to relief and indignation. He threw back his head and laughed more heartily than ever.

"What a pair you are! Frightened of gnats. What else can happen to you?"

The Blackfeet began immediately to pass the time by

running races across the meadow, staging mock fights on horseback, leaping off and on their horses with astonishing ease and swiftness, playing practical jokes on one another, watering their horses in a meandering little stream. They chattered incessantly, gestured and laughed and seemed in jubilant high spirits. They must have enjoyed terrorizing the two ladies, for they kept glancing at them and chuckling.

He sat facing them, his hands on the pommel of his carved leather saddle, heavily decorated with silver. His chest was heaving from the strenuous exertion, his brown skin glistened with moisture. His eyes, as he watched them, were glittering: "You're stubborn, too, I see."

Cherry let go Jacintha's hand and leaped to her feet. Now, as she stood in the carriage, she was at a greater height than he on horseback. Imperiously, she gazed down at him.

"We are stubborn," she proclaimed, and Jacintha watched her with chills of admiration. "We are stubborn and we are loyal. You will not find *us* like the others. We know that we must trust each other. Nothing you can do will change that." Jacintha wanted to applaud.

He, however, only continued watching her and smiling. His eyes were traveling slowly over her body with the assurance of a conqueror. His face looked somber, as if he were plotting further ways to humiliate them.

Jacintha, too, sprang to her feet. "Why don't you let us alone?" she cried, hearing herself first with surprise, then with pride. "We can be happy if you'll let us alone."

At that, wheeling his horse around, raising one arm in a sweeping gesture, and shouting a command in the Indians' tongue, he and the Blackfeet were off at their earlier terrible speed.

The departure was so sudden that Cherry and Jacintha stood for a moment in the carriage and stared after them. Then they turned and looked at each other, puzzled, not altogether sure of what had happened, until all at once they threw their arms about each other and stood embracing and laughing.

"We won!" cried Cherry.

"We won! We won!" they shouted.

They sat down again.

"You see how easy it is?" asked Cherry. "We have nothing to fear from *him*—only from ourselves. He won't do anything to us we don't invite or permit. It's strange," she added reflectively. "That's something I've always known and yet I only realized at this moment."

"How good it makes you feel!" declared Jacintha, and their faces became almost iridescent.

Cherry leaned forward and spoke to the driver who had all this while sat with his slumped back toward them, indifferent to everything.

"Where are they going?" Cherry asked the coachman.

"To the Rendezvous."

"What's that?"

"They were held years ago," explained the driver, "before either of you were dead. He lets them gather now and then for old times' sake. These Indians, of course, not being dead yet but only passing through here, just go for the hell of it.'' He smirked over his shoulder to call attention to his clever remark.

"Are we invited?" Cherry asked.

"No one is invited. Anyone may go."

"Then let's go!"

Once more the lash curled back and the coach bounded forward. They were away on the dusty, eddying trail. Here and there, in the shade, were deep puddles of mud from the recent storms.

"I've heard about the Rendezvous," said Cherry. "There hasn't been one since I arrived, but the old-timers are still talking about the last one." She flared out her fan to whisper behind it. "They say it's incredibly wicked!" She nodded, her dark eyes gleaming with eager naughtiness.

"Is it?" breathed Jacintha. "What do they do?"

Cherry snapped her fan together. "Everything," she stated succinctly.

"Every—" began Jacintha and paused, considering. Then, after a long minute's silence, she clasped Cherry's hand and looked her straight in the eyes. "We musn't go!"

"Whatever are you talking about, Jacintha?"

"We mustn't go!" she repeated, and her voice and body vibrated with conviction. She put one hand against her breast. "I feel it, Cherry, and I know I'm right. If we go, we may destroy everything. Don't you remember that look on his face? This is a trick—a trap he's leading us into. He wants to test us in some way. He is angry with us for having defeated him, and he means to destroy our devotion, once and for all.''

"I thought we just agreed," replied Cherry with an air of cool annoyance, ''that we had only ourselves to fear, not him.''

"We aren't the strongest women in the world," Jacintha reminded her.

Cherry laughed with delight. "No, we're not, thank goodness. Jacintha, for pity's sake, he can't hurt us if we keep our wits about us. I don't believe he wants to hurt us, anyway. It's the difference in our standards that makes us feel pain at what he does. And I don't believe he's angry, either.''

"I'm afraid," insisted Jacintha gloomily. "I'm afraid that he will separate us forever. And I could never bear the loneliness of this place if that happened. Don't forget, it may be a long time before this is over.''

Cherry laughed softly and affectionately. "It may be," she agreed. ''But it will seem even longer if we begin to refuse opportunities for diversion because they may contain danger for us.''

Jacintha was gazing into Cherry's face, her own still full of unhappy foreboding. *How could* they *be good when everyone was being bad?*

Cherry seemed unaware of this dilemma, and Jacintha began to feel that she must be evil herself to worry so much about the possible influence of evil.

"Very well," said Jacintha. "We'll go, and we won't let it destroy us."

And so they continued through the forests and across the meadows, past the steaming, spurting geysers, through the spreading, rushing, warm streams that piddled here and there, and they alternately sniffed the fresh, fragrant pine and wildflowers and the thick, stinking sulfurous vapors. Some of the geysers spouted three hundred feet into the air. Others poked up tentatively like drinking fountains, and sank quiescent once more. They passed warm, shallow pools, colored rust and buff and yellow, and lakes of the purest blue skirting serpentine terraces.

Both women shrieked with laughter to see two black bear cubs, one leaning against a low bank with his paws full of white and yellow daisies, while the other waddled a few steps after their flying carriage and then collapsed suddenly, gazing forlornly after them.

They rounded a corner and there, spreading about the meadows of Roaring Mountain, they saw the Rendezvous site. They were still perhaps a quarter of a mile away, but Cherry called to the driver to stop and let them look for a moment. They were on a slight rise and could see it as though it were an enormous painting of camped armies. To the right rose Roaring Mountain, a thrusting peak, its sides furrowed and whitened, steaming from thousands of vents. From this distance, it appeared to have burned down, turned to ash, and still remained smoking hot. Here and there, vast vaporous steam broke loose and rolled with the wind.

Lemonade Lake lay before them, a shallow yellow-green pool into which had fallen bare, broken trees, rotting in the poisonous water. It seemed as though Lemonade Lake had contested with Roaring Mountain, met defeat, and become this delicate, unhealthy body of water. Nevertheless, the glaring, spewing, glittering white mountain and the sickly little yellow-green lake combined into a gorgeous sight.

Toward the center of the canvas, stretching all the way out of the painting, were wet green meadows. There were small groves of aspen, their leaves glittering in the sun as though a shower of sequins had been cast upon them.

Suddenly Jacintha was jolted by a vision. She remembered the first time she had seen him—resplendent, nearly naked and glorious in the great headdress of white and scarlet feathers.

From the edge of Lemonade Lake, all across the vast meadow and to the foot of the pine-covered mountain, were gathered two or three thousand people, Indians and others, braves, squaws, children, mountain men, and traders. There were hundreds of horses and dozens of dogs. Everything was in motion, running, walking, leaping, crawling, riding, hurrying, lolling, swaggering, prancing; everything was energetically engaged. Even the clouds seemed to go hurrying along.

The tents and tepees of the Indians stood in an irregular circle which straggled around the entire plain, and to each pole a flag was fixed. Horses and mules were gathered, for the most part, at the outskirts, but many were wandering inside, some roaming riderless, others mounted by braves showing off their skill. Innumerable campfires burned, the smoke rising in thin, straight lines.

The squaws wore red calico dresses and white stockings. The Indian men were almost naked or, like the trappers, wore fringed black buckskin. Colored feathers blew and floated everywhere. The sun struck bright, blinding spots off silver bracelets and mirrors hung around squaws' necks.

"It's beautiful!" said Jacintha.

"Isn't it! Driver, go ahead, but slowly."

As they got closer, they heard the noise. Wild war whoops were let out by exuberant Indians. Horses neighed and gave forth piercing, shrill, nervous whinnies. Excited dogs yelped and barked incessantly, prancing about the horses, rolling and tumbling together. Some of the trappers were singing the songs they had brought with them long ago into this new, wild country. Babies cried. Children ran and yelled and shouted deliriously. Drums were being beaten and the sound moved over the vast camp, pulsing like blood through the body of a giant. There was laughter and shrieking, coarse-voiced male bellowing and high-pitched female chatter.

Slowly, their carriage approached.

The Indians' horses were decorated with many-colored beads and glittering metal. Squaws, some of them very pretty indeed and apparently no more than fifteen or sixteen years old, rode bareback and astride, laughing and shouting in loud voices.

It was getting more crowded every moment. Lines of mules passed them, bearing tin kegs, and Cherry said that was the way they transported alcohol in the mountains. From the numbers of mules and kegs, this promised to be a monumental debauch. Indians were still arriving, afoot or on horseback. Their dogs dragged travois loaded with their belongings, and similar contrivances were pulled by horses. Trappers rode alongside, slowly jogging, rough, full-bearded men in greasy buckskin, their eyes showing the peculiar light of men who have escaped civilization and laid hold of their own kind of freedom.

Fashionably dressed men and women from the lodge were arriving in phaetons and Concord coaches, gay and laughing, waving and pointing and calling around. The crowd was now so thick their carriage had come to a standstill.

"Let's get out and walk," said Cherry, who shot her parasol open and climbed down. Jacintha hesitated, then followed her.

"Will you wait for us?" asked Jacintha uncertainly, looking up at the driver.

"I'll be here."

"He doesn't dare go away," said Cherry. "He has his orders. Let's not lose each other."

"Goodness, *no.*"

Holding their parasols, they took each other's hand and set forth into the outer eddies of the burgeoning maelstrom.

"I'm still afraid," said Jacintha, looking warily

about, "that he means this for us."

"Nonsense. I promise you, neither of us has entered his head, except for that one moment back there."

"I'm not so sure," said Jacintha.

She refused to believe the driver's story that these gatherings were held now and then "for old times' sake." The explanation was nothing so simple as that. This was too grand and terrifying a spectacle not to serve some sinister end.

"Remember what you said," she vaguely reminded Cherry.

"I remember, I remember," agreed Cherry, slightly impatient now.

They were aware of being stared at. Heads turned, male and female, Indian and white, as they walked along, making their way among dogs and children, swaggering braves and flirtatious young squaws, wrinkled old men sitting beside their tepees gossiping idly together and smoking. Trappers ambled about, thumbs hooked arrogantly in their belts, throwing out their feet like men accustomed to considerable room in which to move.

Sometimes the two women's passage left a quiet little wake, a toning down of the babble and racket for a moment. They passed a rude mountaineer who gawked and spit a brown squirt of tobacco so close to Jacintha that she jumped aside. He threw back his shaggy head with a burst of ribald laughter.

Gradually, they began to walk a little faster, holding tighter to each other's hand.

Every man they passed was armed. The trappers carried rifles or had knives and pistols stuck in their belts; the braves had bows and arrows and tomahawks slung at their hips.

"Oh, look!" shrieked Jacintha, clutching hold of Cherry's arm and pointing.

"What?"

"That thing! It must be a—"

"*Scalp!*" yelped both women, and started off at a run, away from the tent beside which hung a fresh, bloody scalp. Laughter followed them and scared them so that they kept going, not daring to pause or look back.

As they ran, their fear increased, becoming hysterical as they raced away from an unknown terror. They dodged this way and that, around the tepees, shying from the horses which went prancing by, jingling with bells, waving with feathers, wheeled and maneuvered by proud, naked braves.

They sprinted past rudely constructed stands surrounded by trappers getting drunk on the poisonous brews for sale. These were big, dirty men who poured the liquor down their throats as if they had been thirsty a year, spilling it on their beards, laughing and cracking each other across the shoulders. The ladies darted this way and that to avoid stepping on the Indian children and yapping hounds which swarmed everywhere.

They ran faster and faster, rushing with frantic haste, feeling themselves followed, hovered over, breathed upon. And then they heard a shout: "Hey!" and a form stepped swiftly before them, his arms spread wide to stop their flight. They ran straight into him.

"Grant!"

They stood staring at him and his rude grin, their chests heaving. Slowly, both of them turned and looked around, back to whatever it was they had been fleeing. They saw nothing to fear. Everything was as it had been. Nearby, a group of trappers and Indians squatted on the ground, gambling. Three or four squaws joined them, sitting cross-legged and careless, chattering, bold, and provocative.

Jacintha and Cherry looked at each other and began to laugh. "Aren't we the ninnies!" cried Cherry.

"Afraid of our shadows!"

While they discovered they were in no immediate danger, Grant regarded them sourly. Now he gave one of his harsh, jerking gestures.

"Stop gaping! Come along!" He started off but they hesitated, turning to consult each other's eyes. He glanced back, saw them hesitating, and his face squeezed itself into an expression of outraged fury. *"Come along!"*

"We'd better," whispered Cherry, and they started after him.

He moved nimbly among the tepees and campfires, and between the trading booths surrounded by yelling trappers and Indians bargaining for moccasins and buckskins, coffee and liquor and tobacco. Stinking, bloody beaver pelts, smelling as if they were still raw, stood piled in enormous bundles, and whenever they passed them both women held their noses.

More and more ladies and gentlemen were arriving from the lodge. The gentlemen looked suave and elegant in their Norfolk jackets and knickerbockers of brown plaid, their yellow and brown knitted socks and white linen spats. Others wore lounge suits made of blue serge with wing collars and polka-dot bow ties. The ladies were in gay, garish colors—green, royal blue, purple, garnet, plum, scarlet. Their gowns seemed pasted to swelling breasts and hips, while the skirts were cascading waterfalls of ribbons, tassels, knotted fringe, pleated flounces, bows, and frills. They minced through the meadow on high-heeled, pointed kid slippers, their lifted skirts displaying bright-colored stockings. They carried opened parasols, for the sun was hot and damaging to fine-textured skin, and wore bonnets artfully arranged on elaborate coiffures. Their flirting eyes peeped about with curiosity as they clung to their gentlemen, searching the crowds for the wickedness they had been told to expect. The encampment had begun to resemble the crowded thoroughfare of a great city.

There was a grizzly chained to a stake, restlessly prowling his half-circle, besieged by a pack of snarling wolflike dogs that had succeeded in tearing open his nose and drawing blood from his paws. One of them flew suddenly at him, confident, as if he expected to kill him instantly. The grizzly reared and gave him a swiping blow that sent him hurtling through the air, howling as he went, dead when he landed. The grizzly turned and reared, roaring in a voice that seemed almost a physical explosion, challenging his tormentors. Mountain men, rambling by in their fringed buckskins, stopped to watch and place bets.

Not far away, squaws knelt about campfires, cooking up noisome messes from which Cherry and Jacintha fastidiously averted their eyes.

Even this early in the morning, the camp was acquiring its peculiar characteristic smell: meadow grass, torn and trampled; the ironlike smell of new mud; crushed, fragrant flowers; the decaying flesh on beaver pelts; manure fallen in fresh yellow piles; unwashed, greasy, sweating bodies of trappers and Indians; whiskey, woodsmoke, and burning buffalo chips; the delicate straying scent of pine and fir; boiling coffee—all the swiftly accumulating slop and filth of three thousand humans and twice as many animals.

The sun had moved higher and shone with unusual brilliance. The mountain air was giving both women a dizzy exhilaration that Jacintha had experienced the day she arrived.

As they followed Grant, they began looking around more and more boldly, unable to resist their overwhelming curiosity.

Jacintha was still apprehensive, though. Some of the trappers, all of whom looked like reckless, ungovernable giants to her, were reeling and singing, knocking into each other, grabbing hold of the Indian women who giggled and struggled, looking around for some stern male relative to object or to demand payment.

There'll be trouble before we get out of this.

All at once Grant stopped and pointed. "There he is!" The crowds and tepees were so dense, they had not realized that they were standing at the base of Roaring Mountain.

"Go on!" he yelled.

Looking up the smoking white mountain, they saw him standing on a great jutting ledge, a strange, rocky lichen-covered formation. Though they could not see his face, he was easy to recognize because of his size and the magnificent proportions of his naked body. The way he stood, with his legs spread and fists on his hips, the circle of braves, many of them chiefs with warbonnets, were dwarfed by comparison.

Backs straight and parasols in position, Jacintha and Cherry steeled themselves for the confrontation.

How much simpler it would be if they could see him separately. Or would it? If she went, I would be in agony if I were alone. No, this is better. I would lose my mind if the same thing happened that happened yesterday.

She glanced quickly and covertly from the corner of her eye and encountered Cherry's swift glance. For an instant their eyes met, questioningly; and then they started up the mountainside, picking their way among the rocks between steaming vents, dragging their trains in the white dust. The mountain was so full of activity, hissing and murmuring, sending out boiling clouds of steam and vast whirling vapors, that it seemed it must be about to blow itself wide open.

They ascended slowly, watching their footing but

keeping a wary eye on him. He appeared engrossed in his conversation with the gesticulating chiefs, some of whom wore scarlet military coats of European make, with epaulets and gold lace, trousers and towering shakos. Everyone was in high spirits, and there was much laughter and excited babbling. Apparently they did not consider it necessary to assume for him the rigid bearing and stern decorum they often used to impress white men.

When they were ten or fifteen yards away, Jacintha stopped. Breathing hard with effort, they took out handkerchiefs to dab their foreheads.

"I think we should wait here."

"He must have seen us, even though he pretends he hasn't."

They looked into their mirrors, tilted their heads, touched their curls, straightened their hats, glancing toward him every few seconds. The laughter and talk went on. Cherry and Jacintha could not understand what was being said, as they all talked in some Indian tongue.

Since he continued to ignore them, they began to take interest in the scene below, touching each other on the arm to point out new marvels, pleased and amazed by the whole sprawling panorama. It was much more enjoyable now that they were safely out of it. Even from here the camp was mercilessly noisy.

"Oh, look!" cried Jacintha. "Look at that magnificent horse." She pointed to where a naked brave went prancing proudly by Lemonade Lake on a white horse decked in feathers and bells and ribbons, turning and wheeling in magical obedience to the touch of his rider's knees.

"Look! There's a fight beginning. Somebody's going to get hurt, I know it."

"Look how everyone's running to see it!"

"*Aren't* people bloodthirsty and dreadful."

They were leaning forward, hands on their knees, peering at the fight which, from here, was a twirling kaleidoscope, colors and humans blending and rushing together, when suddenly Jacintha felt a hearty whack on her buttock and cried out in surprise. Cherry was saluted in the same manner, and they straightened abruptly. There he was, smiling down at them.

"How do you like it?" He nodded toward the camp.

He was smiling at Cherry, and Cherry was returning his smile. He was looking at her with speculative intensity, as Cherry's chin tilted provocatively and her face flowered into radiance.

To see them like this, not touching, not moving toward each other, yet so intimate, so unashamedly sensual and luxurious, was an almost unbearable torment to Jacintha. She stood twisting her handkerchief into hard knots and longed to lash out at them both, striking each one so hard they would never again dare to look at each other with that rapt, tenacious ardor.

He does it to hurt me!

No. He doesn't. He does it because he is attracted to

her. And why not? She is using every charm and wile she knows to make herself alluring. While I stand here like a disapproving maiden aunt.

What's the matter with me?

What makes me act like this when I see them together? What happens to change me?

It's her fault! She has somehow made me feel that he is hers because she got here first.

But she told me, didn't she, that she didn't expect me to give him up and knew that I couldn't.

Well, then—

I won't.

Upon this resolution, Jacintha's mouth relaxed and parted just enough to show the edges of her teeth. Her eyes seemed to darken. Her head tipped back so that her throat looked fragile, almost breakable, with the pulse beating at its base. She looked at him, no longer thinking of how Cherry was sparkling and subtly challenging him, but only of how intensely she loved him herself.

After a moment, he glanced down at her. A quick look of surprise crossed his face. Jacintha saw it with exultant pleasure. Slowly and delicately, her tongue moistened her lips. Her head tilted still farther, and her face broke free into a wide, vivid smile, wanton and inviting.

She did not look at Cherry, now that she had this triumphant instant of her own. Jacintha knew that Cherry must be feeling helpless and infuriated.

He smiled and shook his head. "I would pity the man who had to choose between you."

He slipped one arm about Cherry's waist, the other about Jacintha's, and the three of them started down the hill. "Let's take a look around," he said. "You've never seen anything like this before, I can assure you."

Jacintha laughed. "Oh, we know *that!*" she cried, as if she were being very witty. "Don't we, Cherry?" Smiling, she leaned forward to catch Cherry's eye.

Cherry smiled back. "We do, indeed."

Jacintha had found out what she wanted to know. Cherry was angry and Cherry was scared. That meant that she was successful in Cherry's opinion, as in her own. I've won, she told herself. I knew I would, and I have.

But still, she wished she could have a moment to be alone and think about this and to work out what was right and what was wrong.

But there was no time, of course, and no right or wrong, either.

They were descending the mountain slowly and carefully. He attended them like the most courteous gallant, taking first one and then the other by the hand to help them over difficult places, warning them of dangerous spots, smiling and chatting, magnificently at ease within his own fortress. He talked about the rendezvous, why it had originally been held, and how he had decided, after listening to the nostalgic tales of the old trappers, to give them an occasional brief whirl at it.

But Jacintha could not get free of that look she had seen in Cherry's eyes: *I'll never forget it. Never.*

It seemed to Jacintha that the sun was moving across

the sky more swiftly than usual. Perhaps, because everything was new and exciting and dangerous, her sense of time had been lost. She felt herself being hurried forward toward some destination already determined and outside her control.

His hand at their elbows, Jacintha and Cherry were guided through the riotous circus, for it was, beyond doubt, noisier and more unruly than when they had passed through on their way up the mountain.

Time was flying by at an unnatural pace. The horses pranced at a livelier clip. The young braves running races were dashing along as if they had wheels on their feet. The three of them stopped to watch a circle of dancing Indians, their naked bodies painted vermilion and blue and white, animal masks over their heads with horns and feathers and streaming animal tails. They were shuffling and stamping, giving forth sudden terrifying whoops, then raising a sad ululation that quavered outward, to be eagerly seized and imitated by the coyotes.

He led them to a liquor booth about which men stood several deep, shouting and quarreling, laughing and shoving to get at the counter. Cherry and Jacintha hung back, fearful of the drunken men.

He began to shoulder his way among them. They turned at the pressure of his body and, seeing him, parted instantly to give him room. They behaved as though he were a highly respected member of their own clan, yet nothing in their manner suggested that they set him apart as an object of fear. There was comradeship and admira-

tion, but his presence in no way mitigated their recklessness. They must have good reason to believe he approved
of them.

Cherry and Jacintha followed him down the opened
path to the counter; the men shuffled and moved and the
pathway closed. They stood stiff and unmoving behind
him.

The men were close, so close they could not move
without touching them and, cringe and twist as they
would, they could not avoid being jostled. It seemed they
were surrounded by all the men in the world, and would
never get free again. They felt breathless, and within
seconds, their terror had become almost unendurable.

They felt oppressed by a massive, remorseless weight
that seemed to lean in upon them, slowly, steadily, mercilessly, and would soon crush them. Their ears roared with
hideous, stupefying noise, and they shrank from it, closing
their eyes and covering their ears. Worst of all was the
pervasive stench, a rank and musty stink of sweating
bodies and polluted breath, a smell so thick it seemed to
fall upon their skin and clothing in droplets, clinging and
contaminating.

"Have a drink!" Both women glanced up, hands over
their ears, staring at him. He was obviously not only
enjoying this delirious bedlam but was hopeful it would
get even worse.

He seemed both to participate and to remain aloof.

"Come," he insisted, and thrust a half-filled tin cup
at each of them. "Drink it! You both look scared to

death—and there isn't a damn thing here to be afraid of.
Quick! Everything will look different to you once you've
swallowed that.''

Skeptically, like two little girls not convinced the
medicine they are advised to take will do them the good
claimed for it, they lifted their cups and drank the con-
tents in three or four convulsive gulps. The next instant
they burst into fits of coughing and choking and sputter-
ing, gasping as if their throats had been seared by acid. On
every side the men rocked on their heels and roared with
laughter. Finally, when they had more or less recovered,
they stared at him reproachfully.

''What is it?''

''It was poison!''

''I'm going to be sick.''

''No, you aren't. You'll feel much better. Come—
let's take a stroll and see what they're up to. Some of these
fellows are rather ingenious.''

''I can imagine!'' said Jacintha.

The whiskey burned her throat. For a few moments it
filled her with such nausea she was afraid she would not be
able to keep it down. Then the sickness ebbed and she
could feel the heat in her stomach begin to spread and
work outward, through all her body, until the ends of her
fingers began to tingle.

*I like it. He was right. I'm not afraid anymore. I'm
not afraid of anything.*

He and Jacintha and Cherry had emerged from the
mass of men which, only a minute before, had seemed to

hold them captive. The three of them sauntered along, one woman on either side of him, each with her arm linked in his.

They stopped to watch a circle of Indians and trappers playing a game, squatting cross-legged around a heap of objects: strings of beads, buckskin shirts and leggings, fringed doeskin skirts and blouses, mirrors, bells, feathered warbonnets, scalping knives, medicine pipes flaunting feathers and braided ribbons, tomahawks, ruffled silk garters. All attention was focused upon one trapper. He held his closed fists before him, chanting. Now he raised them above his head, swept them around him, shot them out at either side, never once pausing in his monotonous weaving chant, while the others stared avidly, following each gesture, chanting along with him and keeping up a steady, low, hypnotic moan. They looked like drunken participants in some weird religious ritual.

The spell was broken by a sudden furious howl as one of the trappers seized his squaw by the wrist and shoved her onto the pile of gewgaws, as his forfeit. She stumbled and fell and knelt there, waiting passively, watching the man who had resumed his gestures and chanting.

"Don't let him do that!" Jacintha grabbed his arm. "Stop him!"

He ignored her for a moment and then looked down, his face serious and contemplative. He smiled so swiftly that Jacintha blushed and lowered her head while the squaw went to sit beside the man who had won her. They strolled on.

"Look around you," he said. "Things are just warming up. In another hour, there'll be no way of telling who are savages and who are civilized men."

"How disgusting," remarked Jacintha, more from a sense of duty than present conviction. He seemed to realize that and glanced down at her with an amused and tender smile.

But Jacintha was not looking at him. *I'm drunk. I'm actually drunk. Next thing you know I'll be reeling.*

Whatever she looked at was blurred. She might have been underwater, so wavy were the outlines of people and tents and trees. Everyone else looked drunk now, too. Their eyes appeared to be out of focus and their faces lopsided. Her ears rang steadily, so that she could not hear noises as plainly as before. That was a relief. There seemed to be a steady hum, buzzing, vibrating throughout her body. She sailed along quite nicely, independent of her bones and muscles.

It was hot.

Her dress was buttoned to her throat, and she wore many layers of clothing. Impulsively she reached up, took the pins out of her hat, untied the veil and handed it to a passing Indian woman, who received it eagerly and, babbling her thanks, promptly set it upon her greasy black hair. Jacintha tossed back her head and gave it a shake of freedom.

She was beginning to feel as if parts of herself might loosen, jar free, and fall along the wayside. If that happened, she would certainly never find them again. An

Indian would put on whatever it was, as part of his costume.

She leaned against his arm and closed her eyes, feeling the ruthless sun upon her head and face. Oh—she sighed heavily—what do I care?

She heard Cherry's laugh, and that made her eyes snap open. Across his naked chest she saw that Cherry had not only thrown her hat away also, but taken the pins from her hair as well and allowed it to fall in a waving mass over her shoulders and back. Jacintha lifted her arms, removed the pins, and let her own hair fall.

"I'm so glad we came!" cried Cherry.

"So am I!" sang Jacintha.

They were walking by five or six trappers who stood holding great dripping lumps of meat in their hands, sawing and hacking with knives, greedily sucking the cracked marrowbones, smearing their beards and shirts and hands with blood and juice. Jacintha glanced in their direction, saw with horror this filthy repast and, instantly sickened, looked away. At that moment one of the men, who had been gnawing a quivering hunk of raw liver, had it snatched out of his grasp and, with a howl of rage, leaped and sprang upon the other, knocking him to the ground, and they were rolling over and over, locked together. A crowd swiftly began to gather around the clawing, grunting, kicking, biting, snarling men.

They rolled over and over, one on top and then the other. Jacintha and Cherry suddenly and unexpectedly found themselves clinging together, clutching each other as they would clutch a log in a stormy ocean. They stared at each other.

Where is he?

At that moment, a howl of agony rose from one of the men, and they looked back to see the one astride thrust his thumbs into the corners of the other's eyes, give a quick, hard gouge, and the man's eyeballs popped from their sockets. A dog sneaked through and was caught by a man's boot and sent sailing through the air, howling piteously.

Jacintha turned, and before she could stop herself, swung her handbag at the man's head. Her teeth were bared, her eyes blazing; she meant to kill him.

Something seemed to warn him and, the instant before the missile would have struck his head, he whirled and grasped her wrist.

Jacintha found herself captured by a huge, bearded, sweating man who pulled her against his greasy chest and stuck his wet mouth fast upon hers. Feeling as if she had been caught by a grizzly, she began to fight hysterically, her arms flailing out, her head twisting and turning. She planted the heel of her hand against his chin, trying to force his head back, then raked her nails down his cheek. He seized her arm, twisted it behind her, and she heard him laugh.

His breath smelled like rotted weeds in water. His mouth was avid, gnawing and licking at her face and lips, as if he would devour her. She opened her teeth and his tongue plunged into her mouth; she bit down until she tasted blood. He roared and let go of her as she brought her knee jabbing upward into his groin. He howled in rage and pain and gave her a shove so violent that she went sprawling several feet away and landed facedown.

She lay there, feeling the waves of unconsciousness approach and recede, fading, slowly returning. She rolled with them, helpless, hoping to be rescued, then finally gave up and let herself sink to the dark depths.

It seemed that hours went by—though it was no more than a few seconds. Then she rose again to the surface and, with her eyes shut, felt the wet grass beneath her palms and began to explore and stroke it.

Jacintha was relaxed and contented, as if she had wakened early in the morning and happily looked forward to another few hours of sleep. She decided that it must not be grass, after all, but the cool sheets of her own bed. There was Cherry, bending above her. Jacintha began to smile, slowly and peacefully, as she looked up at Cherry.

But Cherry's face, she now saw, was white and tense with anxiety, and the next thing Jacintha knew, Cherry was roughly shaking her shoulder and crying over and over again: "Get up! You *must* get up! Get up, Jacintha—he'll hurt you! *Get up!*" There were tears in her eyes and she began pulling at Jacintha, trying to haul her to her feet.

With Cherry's help, she stood, murmuring, "For a minute it seemed as if everything had been a dream. As if Martin had never shot me and I had never come here . . . "

"Jacintha! We'll both be torn to pieces!"

Now that Jacintha was on her feet, though unsteadily, Cherry began to pull her. "Come! Before he sees us!"

"Where is he?" Jacintha was looking in every direction.

"He's over there! Don't look. He may see you!" Cherry was almost hysterical, running a few steps, returning, trying to drag Jacintha.

But Jacintha had to look. She must see him. She must see what he looked like and what she had done to him. After a few seconds, she found him.

He was huge and ugly and his beard was smeared with dark blood. He was doubled over with his fists jammed into his belly, pumping his legs steadily up and down, his face hideously contorted. He grunted and groaned so loudly they could hear him above the noise.

Jacintha stared at him for an instant, fascinated, feeling some strange and savage satisfaction. Cherry succeeded in almost pulling her off balance, and the two women started running.

They ran as fast and as hard as they could in their clinging skirts, turning their ankles in the pointed high-heeled shoes. Their handbags slung over their wrists swirled about wildly, and a quick-moving Indian severed the cords to Cherry's and held up his treasure, grinning. They kept on without pause, following a devious route toward the outskirts of the rendezvous.

A few trappers and Indians, squaws, and babies slept in the shade of tepees or cottonwoods. Everyone else was noisier and drunker than ever. As they ran, white-faced and wild-eyed, trappers reached out, laughing, to grab hold of their skirts and hair. They twisted away, and their dresses got torn. Complimentary obscenities were shouted. Three reeling mountain men linked hands, trying to capture them, but Cherry and Jacintha ducked under their outspread arms and escaped. Agile and fleet, they ran until they came at last to the camp's edge.

Cherry stretched out on her belly, with Jacintha beside her on her back, arms flung across her eyes. They lay there, speechless, for several minutes.

Finally they recovered enough to sit and look about. They were next to a tepee. An old Indian woman, smoking a pipe, watched with interest, and a naked baby crawled up close and gazed at them in wide-smiling wonder. Tentatively, they smiled back, first at the old woman, then at the baby, and Jacintha reached out to pat the baby's head. Cherry looked for her bag and found only the two tied strings. They combed each other's hair and wiped their wet, dirty faces.

"Well!" said Jacintha finally. "There can't be any doubt about where we are after today!" She got to her feet and tried to smooth her skirts. "I've had enough of this. Let's find the carriage and go home."

She reached down to help Cherry. The breach between them had been completely closed, it seemed, by Cherry's rescuing her.

They were safe here with the baby and the old woman, while all around the uproar continued. It was as if they had found a quiet spot in a battleground. Pandemonium was everywhere about them.

Jacintha lifted her arms and held her hair high to let

the breeze cool her neck. Suddenly Cherry seized Jacintha's arm and pointed in the direction of a hysterical mob.

"Look!"

A few feet away, a trapper had grabbed a squaw around the waist, reached one hand beneath her skirts, and swiftly ran it between her legs. The next instant he gave a yell of rage, picked her up in both hands, lifted her, kicking and protesting, over his head and, with a mighty heave, sent her hurtling through the air. She landed flat on her back, with a crash that seemed sure to break every bone in her body. Even as she struck the ground, Cherry and Jacintha were running forward to help her. And then, since her skirts had been flung high, they stopped with a simultaneous shriek.

"It's a man!"

"Dressed like a squaw!"

"How awful!"

He lay unconscious. A passing trapper gave him a kick. There was noisy laughter on every side, and Cherry and Jacintha turned away.

"We won't even *think* of helping anyone again," vowed Jacintha. "No one in this place wants help anyway."

"We'll only help ourselves," agreed Cherry. "But where is the carriage?"

"Don't *you* know?"

"I have no idea. I was so sure I could find it, but everything's changed since we got here. So many more people have come. Oh, what will we do?"

"We'll find someone from the lodge and ask."

They started walking. There seemed to be fewer lodge guests than before and, whenever they would catch sight of one and start after him, the crowd would swallow him up. Finally, they came upon two well-dressed gentlemen. Eagerly and seriously, gazing up into their faces, Cherry asked them where the coaches were waiting.

The two men looked them up and down, teetered backward and forward, looked at each other, and then suggested that they all have a drink together.

"Don't be impertinent!" cried Jacintha, sure of herself with men like these, even if they were drunk. "Answer our question."

The men simultaneously lifted their eyebrows, smirked, and with elegant though unsteady bows, pointed in what they said was the direction of the carriages. It led back through the encampment.

All the while they were looking for him.

They had not mentioned him since his disappearance, but both were aware of his absence.

Now, though they looked for the carriages, neither intended to leave without seeing him. To search for the carriages gave them something to do.

They both suspected that he was teasing them, that he knew where they were and what they were doing and knew, furthermore, that they were seeking him. For they could feel him. There was an incessant, nagging awareness of his presence. He was a continuing tormenting allurement, dragging them about this maddened meadow, compelling them to wander helplessly to and fro, searching, will-less, as he maneuvered them.

Every tall chief seemed to be he, from a distance. Every crowd must have him at its center.

He may be here—he may be over there.

We may have just missed him.

Perhaps he passed there, while we were looking over here.

"You look that way," said Jacintha, "and I'll look this way. We may miss him if we both look the same way."

There was a sudden piercing scream of warning, quick screams from several others, a rush of thudding hooves, and he came galloping toward them. A path was opened for him—people leaping backward with such skill that there was an illusion of parting waves.

Clamped fiercely between his knees, the stallion halted beside Cherry and Jacintha and reared back, pawing the air, while the two women clung to each other. He slipped down and stood before them laughing.

"Well! Have you found amusement?"

"Oh!" murmured Cherry. "You shouldn't have left us." She stepped easily from Jacintha's clasp and nearer to him, looking up into his face. "We were in terrible danger. Where did you go?"

He pointed off in the distance toward the pine-covered mountain where Indians and trappers were running races on foot and horseback, wrestling and jumping, shooting arrows and rifles. "I went for a breath of fresh air." He glanced back, smiling.

They gazed at him, subdued, admiring, their faces wistful and waiting. Each was thinking: If only he would choose me. If only he would take the initiative, so that I could not be guilty of hurting her.

The squaws looked from him to them, their faces openly envious, their smiles sly and malicious. The women from the lodge looked at him, too, with greedy eyes. A young squaw reached out boldly and stroked one hand across his chest. Three fingers were missing, and the mutilated hand caused both women to shudder as it lay for a moment against his skin.

"What mischief have you been into?" he asked them. His manner was somehow violent, full of the exuberance of strenuous outdoor exertion.

It seemed quite plain to them both as they looked at him—strong, proud, master of himself and them—that he would make no decision for either one, but entertain himself by waiting to see what each was able to contrive.

"We haven't been in any mischief!" said Jacintha. "But we *were* in danger. . . ."

"A horrible beast of a man attacked her and kissed her—"

"Kissed her?"

"I bit him and kicked him."

"Sounds like you've been pretty well entertained."

"Oh, really!" Cherry pouted with playful crossness. "This whole thing is disgusting. It's—it's bestial!"

"It's obscene!" cried Jacintha. "The most vicious things are going on everywhere."

He made a comical grimace of mock surprise. "They

are?'' Then he shook his head. ''There is no such thing as being civilized until you can thoroughly enjoy a return to savagery, now and then.''

They looked at him solemnly, and then slowly shook their heads.

''Oh, no,'' said Jacintha softly.

''You're quite wrong,'' said Cherry.

''You, of course,'' Jacintha informed him, ''would like to destroy civilization. You—being who and what you are—despise everything, since it threatens your supremacy.''

He threw back his head with a sudden burst of laughter. ''I would hate to see your civilization destroyed. I find it a very good show—and that's more than either of you can say for it. You obviously enjoy this very much—or what are you doing here?''

They turned to look at each other, as if for consultation, but found no plausible answer.

''What's this?'' they heard him exclaim, and suddenly he was running with his lithe, easy gait, which seemed merely to skim the earth, toward a crowd gathering with phenomenal rapidity. They were converging from all directions, streaking toward a common center, like bits of metal shot together by a strong magnet.

Cherry and Jacintha caught up and stood behind him near the crowd. There were a man and woman on the ground, the woman beneath with her legs spraddled, the man on top, sawing vigorously back and forth. They looked like one huge, agitated beetle.

Jacintha's mouth fell open, but she was not conscious, after the first astonished moment, of other people about her. The voices, noisy and profane, shouting words and expressions she had never heard before, faded to a distant roar. She was being constantly jostled but, though she accommodated herself to it, regaining her footing when she was given a hard shove, she felt nothing. She stared, glowing hot across her face and throat. She moaned and covered her face with her hands, and when she looked again the man had gotten up and was grinning sheepishly at the crowd and cinching his belt, while the woman sat motionless, hanging her head and looking as if she expected to be beaten.

Jacintha shook herself and looked around for Cherry. She was not in sight, nor was he.

"Cherry!" she cried.

She began twisting and turning, called again and again, her voice becoming more lonely and piteous with each repetition.

"Cherry! Cherry!"

The crowd was breaking up and she found herself painfully aware of everything around her: the moldy smell of the men's greasy shirts; the sour alcoholic taint of their breath; a man's eyes leering at her. She escaped by ducking and skittering away.

The air was chilly, and she buttoned her dress to her throat. Soon it would be dark.

People were moving about as aimlessly as before. She was half running now, peering and searching anxiously.

They were nowhere in sight. They had disappeared.

"Cherry!" Suddenly she stopped still, cupped her hands to her mouth and screamed: *"Cherry!"*

While she had been gawking, they had abandoned her, running to some private place where they could enjoy each other.

It's my punishment. It's what I deserve. I never should have looked. How could I have looked?

A bolt of lightning crossed the sky, and there was a sharp retort of thunder.

"No!" wailed Jacintha, as she lifted her widespread arms and felt a drop of rain pelt her cheek. "No! *Don't!*"

The sky darkened in an instant. It thundered again, a deep and direful sound. Immediately the camp was drenched with a massive, drumming downpour.

The drunken Indians and trappers, laughing and shouting, turned up their faces and opened their mouths and, as they got wet, began to scrub at their snarled beards and hair, rubbing their arms and chests, standing ankle-deep in quickly forming puddles. Jacintha ran into a tepee already sheltering three or four men and women from the lodge. Several Indians were also there, farther back, and the ladies and gentlemen gathered nervously together at the opening of the damp, dark, nasty-smelling tent.

Around her, Jacintha heard them gossiping: "Who do you suppose he's with?" "I saw him only a minute ago, watching that couple." "Where can he have gone?" "He has his hiding places, you know." "Ugh! What a stink this place has—I'd rather get wet!"

"What's the matter with *you*—standing there looking so gloomy?"

This last was addressed to Jacintha. She gave a quick, hostile glance at the man who had spoken. Her face and hair and clothes were wet; her gown torn in many places. She no longer looked like a Victorian lady, but a wild wood creature dressed for a comic masquerade.

She stared at him with a hard, direct gaze and contemptuously shrugged one shoulder.

Many of the Indians and trappers had retired into the tepees. The noise that came from them was louder and more alarming than before. The storm had produced a new frenzy which had made them restless and impatiently lustful.

The man at her side moved nearer and pressed his body suggestively against hers. Jacintha stiffened and closed her fingers around the hilt of a knife left sticking in the lopped-off tree just inside the tepee. She jerked it free and held it tightly in her clenched fist. The gentleman saw her and backed away.

The storm continued. The rain swirled by, accompanied by a moaning sound of wind; thunder crackled and roared. There seemed almost a merry, playful quality about it today.

It grew quieter within, and Jacintha began to have a horrid feeling that if she looked around she might find them all turned into beetles. Softly, she stole out of the tent. She trudged alone through the mud, her skirts filthy, the rain soaking her hair. She felt ugly, with an almost lecherous need to feel uglier still, to look ugly to everyone who saw her—ugly enough to frighten them.

I'm alone. I'm alone now and for the rest of eternity. I shall be miserable. I shall take care never to be anything but miserable. I shall gather up misery and hold it close and slobber over it like that man slobbers over his joint of meat.

The sights around her were no longer horrifying or disgusting but seemed only an external manifestation of her inner feelings. She moved among them almost unconcernedly, taking them for granted.

The storm was waning. The crowds were reappearing, creeping out of their tepees, gathering once more about the liquor booths. She passed men gnawing on maggot-infested meat, drinking melted lard and vomiting it up again, smearing themselves, wallowing in the guts of a great buffalo they were carving. A crowd had set two dogs to fighting and were yelling and betting on the outcome. The canines tore each other to bloody carcasses.

Squaws were getting the fires going again, waving blankets over them, and heavy, sodden smoke drifted through the camp, making eyes burn and smart. In the distance, trees looked like bouquets held in the fist of a hidden giant. The sun came out quickly and very hot, but for only a last few minutes before sinking behind the mountains.

Jacintha had reached the edge of Lemonade Lake and stood gazing into it pensively, one forefinger in her mouth, listening to the ferocious sounds from the encampment and the strange, wistful contrast of a bird on a branch above her head, singing as if to burst his throat. She watched him tenderly. And then she heard a woman's laughter.

She glanced up, looking in every direction, then stepped back instinctively to hide herself behind a fallen trunk. She knelt down, waiting.

She heard Cherry's voice. She would know it anywhere, that same merry, spattering little laugh, which she loved so well.

This was where they had been—together in some secret cave in Roaring Mountain. Hidden from her and from everyone. While she had wandered alone.

She is not my mother anymore. From this moment I reject her. Perhaps she never was my mother. How do I know that she is? I have only her word . . . and his. I think it's all a trick he has played. She is an impostor. She must be!

Jacintha continued to search for them along the edge of Lemonade Lake and up the slopes of the gasping white mountain. She knelt with tense, outstretched fingers before her in the trampled grass. She scarcely breathed.

They might still be in the cave.

She heard the laugh once more. Then Cherry's voice, gay and playful, cried: "I never said that in my life!" And, a short distance up the mountainside, Cherry appeared. She rose into view as if stepping up from an underground hiding place and stood alone for a moment, luxuriously stretching her arms, then folding them behind her head and smiling toward the sky. Suddenly, with a wild and exultant gesture, she flung her arms wide, as if to embrace infinity in her happiness. The white mists shifted about her, making her almost invisible for the next few moments.

Jacintha continued to crouch, watching.

Your mother was no older than you when she died. But she knows a great deal more about men.

The vapor circled upward and, as it lifted, she saw that now he was standing just behind Cherry, one arm about her waist, his hand spread across her belly. He bent his head and kissed her on the mouth. They stood a moment, looking at each other and smiling.

Jacintha sprang to her feet, wanting them to see her. She felt herself swell with hatred.

They came slowly down the mountain, his arm still about her waist, talking softly, laughing continuously. They might have passed her without noticing, so absorbed were they in each other. But when they drew nearer she took a few steps and stood straight in their path, gazing at them with alert, shining hostility.

Cherry gave a start of surprise and the smile disappeared. But as he glanced up, his face was rather grave, and then he smiled.

"Why, Jacintha. Aren't you drenched?"

Cherry had regained her composure and now she was smiling, too, standing beside him as if perfectly confident of possessing him, vibrantly aglow with the extraordinary effect produced by his lovemaking. The look on her face, soft and shining, relaxed and vivacious, struck Jacintha as a physical blow. Her body was easy, composed, secretly enfolding the spreading, pulsing warmth he had left her.

At that moment Jacintha remembered the knife she still held in her right hand.

The three stood staring at one another, motionless and silent for several moments. Jacintha grew increasingly nervous and eager. She trembled and shook, and suddenly the need for action became uncontrollable. She started toward them, filled with hatred, hoping and expecting to destroy them both. She believed at that moment she had strength and rage enough for any act.

As she started to move, he came slowly toward her, Cherry walking at his side.

Slowly, one step and then another, they shortened the distance between them. Cherry's expression was changing. The radiant confidence and languid contentment had passed into curiosity and was now becoming sad, poignant pity. As they drew nearer, Cherry impulsively held forth her hands and opened her mouth to speak.

It was the look of pity on Cherry's face that made Jacintha, uttering a strange, deep moan, start to run, moving lightly and swiftly, eyes gleaming. As she reached them she swept back her arm, held the knife poised for an instant, then brought it sweeping downward. Cherry screamed, and inadvertently, Jacintha changed the direction of the blow, flashed it sideways—envisioning how it would tear open his face and throat.

For a fraction of a second she was fixed greedily upon

that vision. She shut her eyes, then felt a blow across the side of her face, the knife flying out of her hand like a hummingbird. She fell at his feet.

Cherry turned to him. "You knew she was hysterical! You've hurt her!" He gave a look of warning and shook his head.

Cherry knelt, tenderly raised Jacintha's head and held it cradled against her breasts, rocking gently backward and forward, crooning, "Darling, my darling Jacintha, speak to me. He didn't hurt you, did he? Forgive me."

Jacintha lay with her eyes closed. The hatred was gone. A tear splashed onto her face, causing her vaguely to wonder why Cherry should be crying.

It was dark now, and as he stood looking down at them, he seemed to rise gigantically, filling the night itself. They were small and helpless, delicate creatures who could no more challenge him than could Lemonade Lake challenge Roaring Mountain.

Across the encampment, dozens of fires smoked, and sparks shot toward the sky, appearing to mingle with the stars emerging in miraculous quantity.

How I hate myself. I wish it had been possible for him to kill me. I would kill myself, if I could. I am nothing of what I pretended to be.

She considered these things in a detached and philosophical way, with only mild concern. She felt that she had had an important revelation, one which would change all the future for her.

At last, slowly, she opened her eyes and looked up at

Cherry, who still crooned and rocked as Jacintha considered her reasons for self-hatred. Cherry burst into tears and began repeatedly kissing her face.

"Oh, Jacintha. Forgive me."

Jacintha looked at her, marveling that it was Cherry asking her forgiveness, when his voice spoke sharply:

"Leave her alone, Cherry! And get up!"

Cherry looked swiftly about. He stood motionless, an awesome black shadow against the smoking white mountain that murmured and hissed behind him and shone in the dark like silver. She stared at him defiantly.

"Get up!"

"You've hurt her. She isn't able to speak."

He leaned down, seized Cherry by the shoulders and yanked her to her feet. With a cry of anger she tried to pull away from him and return to Jacintha, who was now sitting up, her palm against her face; it did not hurt at all. Cherry struggled to rejoin her, but he held her fast, and the next instant, a shrill whistle sounded above the camp's riotous noise.

In what seemed only seconds, they heard a clattering of hooves and racketing of wheels, and their carriage drove swiftly toward them and stopped. He pitched Cherry into it, still violently protesting:

"I won't leave her! I won't leave her alone with you! I won't—"

"Shut up!" He spoke sharply, but without real anger, like a stern parent to a troublesome child. "Drive a hundred yards or so along the path and wait." The driver snapped his whip and they were gone.

"Don't you dare hurt her!" Cherry cried once more. Then she could be seen no longer, and the noise of the carriage was drowned in the din from the camp.

Jacintha had not even glanced up as Cherry was put into the carriage and sent away. Now she waited and felt herself willing to accept whatever he would do with her. Both were silent for several moments.

All at once Jacintha covered her face with both hands. "I don't care," she whispered. "I don't care what you do. I couldn't help myself...."

His hand touched her shoulder, and she glanced up in a sudden terror that belied the listless words.

"I won't hurt you," he said softly. "I'm sorry if I hurt you a moment ago—but there wasn't much time." His voice sounded faintly amused, though it was too dark to see his face. Now he bent, slipped his hands under her armpits, and drew her slowly and gently to her feet. He held her against him. Helpless and stunned, her heart beating fast with fear, she stood stiffly, waiting. She did not doubt that he would do something terrible to her, and that he was enjoying her agony of suspense.

He continued to hold her against him, and very carefully, slowly, tenderly, his hands stroked her hair, her back, her arms, her face. The caresses were infinitely soothing, almost healing, she felt, and without sensuality. Trustingly, she relaxed, closed her eyes, rested against him and found herself being slowly restored to her normal strength, serenity, self-confidence. The pleasure was great, though not voluptuous, and she wanted to linger there forever, shut into this dark, private world, aware of nothing but the continuous, slow movements of his hands. She sighed.

Then, still with great care, he released her and, to her surprise, she found herself standing alone, only a few inches from him, though it seemed a great, cold distance was between them. Alarmed, she moved toward him.

"Go back with her," he said.

"Go back?"

"Go back to the lodge."

"I want to stay with you."

She tried to see him, but it was too dark. He was only a dim, massive figure before her, and a powerfully felt presence. Even more, she wished that he could see her, for she felt that her beauty might persuade him where her words could not.

"Let me stay with you. I won't ask for anything or expect anything. . . . ''

Having defeated her, now he was obliged to be responsible for her—or so she believed.

They heard a restless trampling nearby, and Jacintha started nervously. "What was that?"

"My horse. Go on—go back." He sounded impatient.

"But I—"

"Good-bye."

He turned swiftly, and she saw his vague shadow mount the black stallion. He raised one arm to her in salute, and was off at a furious gallop, down the forest pathway, away from the rendezvous. Jacintha stood and stared. Now there was nothing, not even the sound of his horse galloping away.

The noise from the camp blasted in her ears, and she covered them, cowering. Then she began to run toward the carriage. The dark was suddenly populated by a hundred hostilities. Indians creeping toward her, prowling wolves, trappers insanely drunk, tremendous bears, silent mountain lions. She ran as fast as she could. She began to call Cherry's name, calling louder and more wildly when there was no answer.

Then Cherry must have heard her through the noise. "Jacintha! Here I am! Jacintha!"

Finally she got to the carriage and stood beside it, panting. Cherry reached down and took her hand.

"Where is he?"

"Gone. He rode away."

"What did he do to you?"

"Nothing," Jacintha said, her voice soft and light and bewildered. "He was kind to me. I think he pitied me." She felt lost, powerless, deprived of everything but the need to be with him. She was shivering and realized that it had grown very cold.

"Get in," said Cherry. "It's freezing here at this time of year. The nights are always cold. Let me bundle you up." She was wrapping Jacintha in a buffalo robe, lined with scarlet wool. She told the driver to take them back to the main lodge.

The two women sat side by side, close together, with arms linked and hands clasped. They were silent for what seemed a long while, rushing through the darkness.

Cherry was the first to speak. "Will you be able to forgive me, Jacintha?"

Jacintha gazed steadily ahead. "I would have done what you did."

Cherry gave her hand a warm, grateful pressure. "How honest you are! I'm proud of you. But I am ashamed of myself. I should have been able to be less selfish."

"I don't think so. Considering what he is, how could you be?"

"Look! What's that?"

They looked up as Cherry's hand darted forth and seized a snowflake; it melted as she touched it. And then they saw great, soft, floating flakes, circling overhead, aimlessly drifting, and settling upon the trees and earth.

"Does that mean the same thing a rainstorm does?" asked Jacintha hesitantly.

Cherry laughed. "No. It means something quite different. It means that he has gone away."

Jacintha sat up straight, a quick flash striking the back of her neck and then the pit of her stomach. "Gone away!"

"Not forever," said Cherry soothingly. "He always leaves at this time of year. We'll be snowed in, you know, for months."

"He'll be gone for months? Oh, no!"

"He'll return in the spring. Or, if not this next spring, then perhaps the following one. Someday, at least, he will come back." Cherry's voice was warm as she spoke, saying the words slowly, as if to accustom Jacintha gradually to the shock. "Until he does," she added, "we shall comfort each other."

Jacintha was stupefied. It was the one thing she had not expected. Almost nothing else could have surprised her now, but she had never anticipated his prolonged absence. After all, this was his domain, was it not?

"Why does he go?" she asked finally.

"No one knows *why* he does anything." There was a brief pause, and Cherry added, "You will be surprised at how lasting those memories are."

Jacintha felt her face grow red. "Will I?"

Cherry's voice was gay and cheerful again, and it seemed she had quite recovered from the confusion and exhausting excitement of the day.

No matter what happened, it seemed, Cherry's natural gaiety and resilience would reassert itself.

Jacintha had a picture of them together during the months ahead: Cherry busy and lighthearted, chattering and merry—while she sat forlornly brooding, waiting.

"Jacintha, darling," continued Cherry, "don't be sad. We'll have so many things to do. Why, we'll make spatterwork lampshades and pretty little boxes out of bark and leaves. We'll be together. We'll entertain each other, won't we?"

The snow was settling steadily, falling thicker and

thicker. The trees were fringed with white and the earth was white. The air was both cool and warm.

Like death, thought Jacintha. As I remember it.

"Yes," she agreed, sadly. "I suppose we will." She turned to Cherry again. "Where does he go?"

"I don't know." Cherry and Jacintha were silent a moment, and then Cherry's hand closed over Jacintha's. She spoke with soft tenderness. "In life, men think of many things—while women, once they have the appetite for it, think of only one: *When?*" She paused. "It's no different here."

Jacintha shrugged. "I love him. Isn't that ridiculous? To love a man who can never love you?"

"But you must not judge him as we judge the men of our world," Cherry said consolingly. "Love is not possible to him. And what difference does it make? He understands the ingredients of our kind of love well enough to make us love him. That's a great deal more than our men were able to do."

Jacintha turned and looked at Cherry. Their faces were close, their hair rose about their heads, flying in the wind. Their dark eyes gazed with steady intensity.

Jacintha shook her head. "But he chose *you*—not me."

"Perhaps—perhaps not. Eternity isn't over yet, you know." Cherry laughed gaily. "Come, darling—" She hugged her again. "We must do what we can to comfort each other. I waited for him alone before—you wait *much* longer, that way."

Jacintha glanced away, ashamed of her self-absorption. Then, quickly and impulsively, she smiled and kissed Cherry's cheek. "We'll be so happy together," she declared, "that we won't care if he comes back or not!"

"Of course we won't."

Cherry reached up and swiped with one cupped hand at the snowflakes. "Look!" she cried with delight. "I've caught a dozen of them. Here . . ." And very carefully, concentrating earnestly, she tried to pass them to Jacintha, who gave her entire rapt attention. When the snowflakes escaped, they began eagerly grabbing for others, standing in the carriage, their laughter ringing out in the dark, cold night.